Lillian Hinman Shuey

Don Luis' Wife

A Romance of the West Indies

Lillian Hinman Shuey

Don Luis' Wife
A Romance of the West Indies

ISBN/EAN: 9783744770873

Printed in Europe, USA, Canada, Australia, Japan

Cover: Foto ©Andreas Hilbeck / pixelio.de

More available books at **www.hansebooks.com**

Don Luis' Wife

A Romance of the West Indies

From Her Letters, and the Manuscripts of the
Padre, the Doctor Caccavelli, Marè
Aurèle, Curate of Samaná

By

Lillian Hinman Shuey

*Author of " California-Sunshine," verse, and " David of
Juniper Gulch," a Novel*

VT CRESCIT

Lamson, Wolffe and Company

Boston, New York and London

MDCCCXCVII

████████on, Wolffe and Company.

───────

███████████ights reserved.

Norwood Press
J. S. Cushing & Co.—Berwick & Smith
Norwood Mass. U.S.A.

Preface

SHORTLY before the death of the Doctor Caccavelli at Samaná, his manuscripts relating to the Señora de Curzoñ were, at his request, sent to California, to the parties who naturally would wish to care for and preserve them. They, together with the letters which I here reproduce in part, have been stored for a number of years in a safe-deposit building in San Francisco.

The story which I present from these manuscripts contains the true account of the experience and adventures of a New England girl as the wife of a gentleman of fortune on the Island of San Domingo.

It illustrates some of the intricacies that entangle the fate of an American woman who marries a foreigner, especially one of

rank and fortune ; and introduces to public approbation several persons from actual
life, whose noble qualities I have in no
way overstated.

Contents

" FRIAR.   Bound by my charity and my blessed
        order,
I come to visit the afflicted spirits
Here in the prison : do me the common right
To let me see them ; and to make me know
The nature of their crimes, that I may minister
To them accordingly."

SHAKESPERE.

" Ah, Richard ! with the eyes of heavy mind
  I see thy glory, like a shooting star,
  Fall to the base earth from the firmament.
  The sun sets weeping in the lowly west,
  Witnessing storms to come, woes and unrest :
  Thy friends are fled to wait upon thy foes ;
  And crossly to thy good all fortune goes."

SHAKESPERE.

" For charity itself fulfils the law :
  And who can sever love from charity ? "

SHAKESPERE.

Don Luis' Wife

Chapter I

Memoranda of the Padre Caccavelli

(Translated from the Spanish)

EVER since I went to see her that day, "pauvre petite infortuné," and she, with her soft dark eyes swimming with tears, begged me to be her friend, her only one then, seemingly, in this faraway island, I have tried to be her protector, as far as my conscience would allow, and as far as was consistent with my sacred office.

I like to think of her character and virtues, as she was the only American woman I ever knew well; and her manners and accomplishments were pleasing to me; as there are no women like her among the Spanish and native women of Samaná.

She was so grateful for all the little things I was able to do for her, and I, in turn, was pleased to know all she told me of that great country, the United States. As I have noted her vivacity, her gentleness, her talents, her fidelity, and depth of soul, I have had a worldly feeling of thankfulness, that I was permitted to hold such intimate relations to her, by grace of my profession as physician, and my position as curate of Samaná.

As I had, during my first interviews with her, so much difficulty in understanding the pure English she spoke, I asked her to write for me a true and detailed account of her meeting with and marriage to the Count of Villemaceda; and of her experiences before she came to Samaná, in order that I might study it over carefully, and come to a better understanding of the remarkable circumstances.

And truly she wrote it all out plainly for me, and with the pure honesty of heart with which she might have written it for that noble and venerable mother in her New England home in Northham, Maine.

I take it out sometimes and read it over, for it is a chapter of happiness and love, such as comes not often to my knowledge; the confessions that come to me mainly are those of sorrow, cupidity, and guilt. And then it pleases me to dwell upon it, for it is a great bar of golden sunlight falling into the blackness of the shadow that covered most of her life in Samaná.

And so, before I laid it away with my other notes of her life here, lest it be contaminated with the sorrows of them, I marked it plainly, "The Happiness of the Countess of Villemaceda."

Her Account of the Happiness

I was born, good Padre, the curate, in the old New England town of Northham, Maine; and, with the exception of occasional winters in New York city, I lived there till my marriage with Don Luis, the Count of Villemaceda.

My father was a teacher of the classics, a professor in Northham College; he passed away some years ago, but my

white-haired mother and my laughing,
loving sister Nell are there in the dear
old homestead on the sunny slope of the
hill, which overlooks the straggling town.

I can look back now and say that I
was always happy — just a careless, half-
spoiled child. My dear father loved me
too well, and often when I would go to
him in the cosy library at home with my
lessons, he would kiss me and detain me
with caresses, when he would better have
ordered me away with a frown.

When my sister Nell graduated, I did
not go to the college any more, because
I could take my French and music as
well at home, and there was my painting,
which I liked best of all.

Then mamma needed me, because Nell
had so much company, and there were
college people to dine some days every
week. Then all the village people loved
mamma, and there was only I to help her,
when any of them were sick or in trouble.

The door of our dear old elm-shaded
home was always swinging one way or the
other, and it was always I to run and

open the door, with merry words to make them welcome; or to linger on the steps, and at the gate, to speed them away with our love and thanks, for we valued all our friends.   How could it be otherwise? Father had been in the college twenty-five years, and the people were many of them children of his own college friends.

Dear father's Phi Beta Kappa medal is pendant from my necklace now, and it is the only ornament I have the heart to wear, since I have laid aside the splendid diamond ring I wore when I landed at Samaná.

To think of it all now, I seemed to have always lived in a whirl of home and village pleasures.

There were all the Christmases to make merry, the New Years to make happy, and all the Commencements to help render pleasant; there were picnics and boating, drives, sleigh rides, sketching days, and pictures to finish for friends; the old home must needs be kept cool and inviting in summer and warm and cosy in winter, and then there were friends who expected us to visit them.

Nell loved her books, and I loved to see her growing so learned and dignified and bookish. I like those kind of people; I have always worshipped people who know ever so much more than I do.

It was strange — Nell's many beaux always turned to me for comfort, when they found that Nell was looking far away over their heads. Not many of them proposed to me, however, for I let them plainly see that I didn't want what Nell wouldn't have.

And I suppose that was the reason that I grew not to think of the Northham young men for myself, for Nell was beautiful, and they all liked her.

After father died it was so different for a while! Then when the Burnets came from New York and fitted up a country place at Northham, they took to Nell, of course, and we were invited there, and began to see a great many New York people. It was there that I met Luis de Curzoñ, Count of Villemaceda, as you say I should call him. Mr. Burnet, you know, was one of the New York merchants, through whom Don Luis made his purchases for his warehouses here. The Burnets were very much pleased, as all the village people well knew, when Don Luis accepted an invitation to come to Northham as a guest at the Burnet " Villa," for so they began to call their handsome home about this time.

Mrs. Burnet had so often depended on Nell and me to help her with her company, that we thought nothing unusual when she sent up a note one afternoon saying that a titled gentleman from the West Indies would be up from New York that evening, and asking us to come down to tea. As had been our habit, we dressed in our best, hurried down the hill alone, and slipped in at a side path, through a tangle of bare tree branches ; then after a moment to unwrap, we were ready to go into the dining-room.

This afternoon, in particular, I saw that Nell was in her best ; I had mended her black laces, cascaded them about her shoulders, and rolled her hair high on her proud head. I had been so busy

with her, that I had had time only to slip
into a soft gray silk with a long train;
and my hair, I let it curl as it would, and
gave the rest a twist.

Mrs. Burnet met us in the little side
hall and hurried us into her room. She
drew down Nell's proud head and kissed
her white brow.

"Nellie Wright," she said proudly,
"this is your chance; we planned this all
for you. He is a rich merchant, and a
sort of count, I believe. His New York
letters are sent to Mr. Burnet for the
steamer, and they are addressed either,
'Monsieur de Curzoñ' or 'Don Luis
de Curzoñ' or 'Luis, Count of Villemaceda'; and oh, he's such a charming
man! Mr. Burnet is just wild over him."
All this she said so rapidly, that we could
only stare at her as she went on.

"And he said to me yesterday, — 'I
wish we could get Nell Wright for Mr.
Curzoñ. Wouldn't she make a stun-
ning countess, or doña, or whatever we'd
call her? We'd all get out to the islands, and they say Curzoñ entertains in

fine style in New York.' Now, Nell, do your best; we won't be getting many more chances like that for you." Then she turned to me, —

"How's mamma, to-night, Paula? How pretty you look, dear."

Well, we went in, and were presented to Mr. Curzoñ at table. And, you know, good curate, how dignified and impressive he can be. I noted his strong, keen, gray eyes, his broad shoulders, the noble poise of the head, and then somehow, I seemed all in a flutter and confusion. I tried to talk to Mrs. Burnet, but I was hearing all the while his rich, easy tones, as he was speaking to Mr. Burnet about Thiers and French politics.

I heard every word he said, for all handsome Emerson Paine was sitting opposite, smiling and talking to me to attract Nell's attention.

After tea, Mr. Burnet gave his arm to Nell, Mr. Curzoñ bowed to Mrs. Burnet, and I followed with Emerson, being merry with him to cheer him, for I knew he admired Nell. I took my place on the piano stool to free him, so that he could follow Nell. I rested my fingers softly on a few chords.

Suddenly a tall form cut off the bright light, and the very air next my cheek seemed warmer and softer. I turned with a start to look up into the face of Mr. Curzoñ, as he was bending over me. He seemed to shut out the room and all the rest. His presence was so powerful, so strangely absorbing.

Somehow, all at once, I was no longer little Paula Wright, but another woman, with a new, unfamiliar destiny; and I felt powerless, even then, to resist the influence that drew me, heart and soul, away from my careless, happy self into the strange world of my new love, for so I must tell you, dear Padre, it was even then.

But I felt at that moment only stunned, amazed.

He began first by asking me when I would be in New York, and then he found a song I knew, and very soon he was singing with me in his rich, low tenor.

What an evening that was! Nell and Emerson came and sang too.

Afterwards, we talked about art, and they all praised some roses I had done. Then he talked of art in Paris and Berlin, and my heart almost stood still to have the grand things I had dreamed of brought so near to me. He brought everything before my eyes. How abashed I felt over my poor little pictures!

When he arose and walked into the library with Mr. Burnet, I had to rouse myself with an effort, Emerson and Nell were in such a hurry to go.

After that, dear Padre, I cannot explain it all.

Mr. Curzoñ was very attentive to Nell, and the Burnets encouraged him in every way they could.

But his attentions to Nell were only for courtesy after all; but Emerson Paine and I did not know. We used to be together a great deal in those days, and we were so very gay with each other, that Nell used to stare at us with red spots in her cheeks; but the count regarded us serenely. Whenever the count found a chance to talk to me I used to be so fluttered, and shy, and nervous, that I was glad to escape away to Emerson. And then it was fun to tease Nell.

One cold frosty morning, Emerson came and took me for a drive in his new little cutter. I teased him all the way, poor jealous boy! When he left me, rosy and gay at the gate, I knew by the parted curtains in the parlor that some one was there.

I entered the house softly, and when I came into the room next to the parlor, the door being ajar, I stopped and looked in, transfixed by what I saw.

My mother was sitting in her great chair, where the soft sunshine fell full on her white curls and calm, patient face.

Don Luis was sitting close beside her, and was holding one of her still white hands. He was speaking in a low tone, and she was listening silently. They did not see me, and his clear words came to me:

"I will be a good husband, dear madam. I will not disappoint you."

My fur cap fell from my grasp, and I went on through the house to find Nell.

She was in the kitchen with Rhoda, the girl, fretting over the lunch. She looked down at me with hot cheeks.

"Well," she said, "are you happy now? He went tearing off, without waiting to speak to me."

"No," I said, feeling numb all over. "He's in the parlor now, asking mamma for you."

"Emerson?" she cried.

But I had sunk down in a wretched little heap on the floor. She began to shake me.

"Oh, you little dunce! Somebody's in the parlor asking mamma, but not for me — for you — for you! Don't look so, Paula; rouse up and help me with the lunch. You ought to once more, if you are going to be the Countess of Villemaceda."

But I ran off to my room, and curled down with a throbbing heart in the red cushions of my settee.

After a while mother came in, slowly and quietly. She put her hand in the curls of my hair, and kneeling, kissed the bit of cheek that I uncovered.

"Darling," she said, "do you want to go with this strange man, and be his wife, in a foreign country?"

I only caught her hand and was silent. Mamma waited, then she said:

"There is only one reason, dear child. He may be talented and titled. He may be well off. He says he has made and lost a fortune, and is now about to make another. He may be as good and generous and as kind as he seems; but with all that, there is but one reason why you should marry him, and that was the reason I had to marry your father — do you love him, Paula?"

My dear, foolish, romantic old mother! Then I sprang up and clasped my arms about her, and sobbed on her warm heart.

She was so innocent and good! She could not think of any other reason. Her pure heart was too noble.

Don Luis did not stay to lunch, and

Nell brought tea for me up to my room. She sat down in a low chair, and clasped her hands over her head.

"*Are* you going to keep us in suspense any longer?" she said.

I was sitting up straight to drink my tea.

"What suspense?" I cried.

She looked down, flushing.

"Well, of course, if you go away, it would be nice for, for—"

"For Emerson to come here and take my place," I said hastily.

She came and encircled me with her arm.

"You wouldn't care, would you?"

"Not if I go," I said. She kissed me and went out. I was no longer anything to her: it was only Emerson. Then, for the first time, I was glad that this strange fascination of love had come to me also; and I was really willing and anxious to give my whole heart, my trusting, foolish, little heart, to the tall and handsome Don Luis.

The next day I went out alone with

Don Luis, for the first time. He had the finest horses in Northham; and as we glided over the low white hills, among the dear familiar scenes, it seemed as if all the world had opened up into a radiant heaven for me. I was happy, and Don Luis seemed to know it. But he was so courteous and considerate! He did not offer me any rude caresses, but only once folded me to his breast, and softly kissed my brow.

He told me of Genoa, where he was born of Spanish and French parentage; of Paris, where he had been educated; of Italy, and of his father's estate in Spain, which a distant relative held, until it would be convenient for him to claim it. He told me also of his large, roomy, palm-shaded house at Santa Barbara de Samaná, close by the sea; and of his great warehouses near by.

Then he told me of the dark-eyed doña, who had been his wife in his early youth; of her child, a boy, who had grown up, and at twenty had married a rich Spanish heiress of the far south island of Curaçoa. Only a few months previous the son had died, and the rich Spanish girl was a widow with a child.

"So I am a grandfather at forty," Don Luis said, smiling at me.

"And the dear babe?" I said.

"Oh, I have not seen him, but we shall when we go to Curaçoa. He has a rich grandfather there, a man of considerable importance, the Señor Hippolite Lavandier, who watches over him, with a jealous eye, because, forsooth, he is sole heir to all his property. But we must not disturb our happiness by thinking of those things, Paula. Let us talk of my new future,—my English future, I will call it, with my fair, refined American wife. My life will be rich now, royally rich, with books, and art, and the true companionship that birth and education affords. Will it not be so, Paula?"

Then, with tears in my eyes, I told him, that I would try to make his life and home so full of joys and comforts that he would forget all his barren and wasted years.

c

I was so happy, when he gravely kissed my hand, and left me in our hall. I ran in, and tearing off my wraps, I sank at my mother's feet, and thanked her for her generous consent; for I was her pet, if Nell *was* her pride, and she could not but be lonely with me far away on the islands of the sea. My dear mother! It was a sacrifice, for she trembled and grew pale when I first began to speak of getting ready to be married. But she showed her true heroism, and put her own bereavement back in her heart, when she saw how happy I was, and how lively and business-like Nell had suddenly become.

For Emerson, if he was not very rich, was the only man north of Boston good enough for Nell.

Chapter II

They Say " Bon Soir, Madame to the " Doll-Bride "

(The Happiness continued)

AND so it was immediately announced that we were to be married, and very soon.

You cannot imagine, good Padre, the excitement this created in Northham and vicinity, where every one knew us, and we knew every one. My friends from far and near came rushing in unceremoniously to ask questions. But they found me so busy I could not answer them; Nell and I left that to mother, while we helped the village dressmaker with my dresses.

Meanwhile, our lawyer, my father's dear old friend, Judge Bacon, had written to New York, and found out that Mr. Cur-zoñ was indeed all he represented himself

19

to be, and there came so many letters of recommendation from mercantile people, that I told Nell I would read no more of them.

I was not marrying him for his money, and as I had none myself, I saw no need of such formalities. Then Mr. Burnet had been out to San Domingo, and I felt that his recommendation was enough.

But as Don Luis could not delay on account of his business, he gave me but two weeks to get ready in, and this was what so excited my friends. They all brought their presents without waiting for the day. They were not rich presents, for none of us are so very wealthy in Northham, but they represented stores of love and good wishes; and the parting tears dropped over the little packages were lovelier to me than pearls and diamonds.

For, although Don Luis had promised to bring me home for a summer visit, yet to go to the islands of the West Indies seemed to us village people almost like going out of the world.

The day before the wedding, Emerson

came with his sleigh and dashing team to
take me to see my aged friends who could
not come out to see me.

A little snow was whitening our caps,
but it was grand sleighing, and our ponies
threw up their proud heads and seemed
to have caught the spirit and excitement
of the day. I made short calls and kept
cheery through it all. Everywhere it was
"God bless you, Paula," and "Good-by,
dear little girl," and "Don't forget us,
dearest," and then I would hurry out. It
was unreal, like a swift dream, and I was
too happy to realize that I was taking a
long farewell of my beloved friends.

At nine o'clock, on the 9th of March,
we were married like any one else. The
house was full of friends, all with kind
congratulations and tender "good-bys";
and a party of them went with us on the
train to West Junction. It seemed as if
they would lose no chance to let this
dignified foreigner know how much they
valued "little Paula." It seemed a little
strange to see them go back; and I
began to realize that Don Luis would

have to be everything to me in place of the dear old homestead, my mother, and Nell, and all these friends.

So I nestled against his shoulder as the train rushed on to New York, and thought of what he had said to my old friend, Jack Graves.

Jack had come forward to congratulate him, and looking very serious, too, for Jack had wanted to marry me once. Jack said:

"You must take good care of Paula, Mr. Curzoñ."

"Of course I shall," Don Luis replied; "she is only a little doll-wife to love and admire." But Jack pulled his mustache, and said solemnly:

"But you will find she isn't stuffed with sawdust, Mr. Curzoñ." At this we all laughed. Jack is so queer. Had he been a little less queer, I might have liked him more. Poor Jack! And now I know you are saying "poor Paula," too, my good Padre.

I felt like a countess, indeed, when we reached those lovely rooms in a New

York hotel the next morning. It was bitter cold in New York that day, but the rooms were bright and warm with fires, and Don Luis had telegraphed ahead for flowers and some rare California fruits; there was a little colored maid to wait upon me.

In the afternoon we received Don Luis' friends — all gentlemen, and all French. I had thought myself but a doll, a child-wife, and I was surprised indeed to hear myself called " Madame."

They seemed to approve of me; they smiled upon me and bowed very low; they all took wine, talked a great deal to Don Luis, took more wine, and then bowed themselves out, with " Bon Soir, Madame," to me.

I was glad when they were all gone, for I could not understand their rapidly spoken words.

Then Don Luis took me in his arms and kissed me more lovingly than ever before.

" You have played your part well, Paula petite," he said; " you please me in everything you do."

Oh, my noble Catholic friend! Those were great words. And I shall ever believe, to my dying day, that he meant them.

Chapter III

The Statue of Empress Josephine

(The Happiness continued)

THE next day we went to dine with one of the French gentlemen in a beautiful home, filled with the most choice and artistic pictures and articles of virtu I had ever seen. I was royally treated by those charming people, and Don Luis was very happy aiding me in my conversation.

The day after that we took a carriage and went to Stewart's to fill up my trunks with things suitable for a tropical climate; and indeed, good friend, had I not been there to restrain Don Luis' lavish hand, "the doll's" wardrobe would have been absurdly elegant. I was truly amazed and surprised when I saw the brass bedstead, with the blue silk canopy

25

and hangings, that he had ordered shipped by the barque *Thetis* to my new island home.

But Don Luis only smiled and said I would be the first lady of Samaná, and that I would need just such handsome things.

I think that must have been the coldest day New York ever knew.

When I returned to our rooms, I stood watching the frozen expressions of the throng going up and down Broadway, hurrying to get out of the cold, piercing winds.

In the afternoon Don Luis said that he ought to go to see a sick friend in Elizabethtown, but that he disliked to leave me alone so long. I begged him to go, then curled myself up in an easy chair before the blazing coals, with a book, and my tender thoughts of the dear ones in the old homestead, and my loving friends in Northham; but my thoughts would wander to my new island home, and how I would be received in that strange land.

Don Luis had told me of his plans, and I could then think them over definitely.

Business had arisen which called him to Martinique; and my heart was filled with pride to know that I was to see the birthplace home of the famed and beautiful Empress Josephine. We were to go on a merchant ship, whose captain was a friend of Don Luis.

We were to sail from here to the Dutch island of Curaçoa, where Don Luis said he had some affairs to arrange, and where we would meet his little grandchild, Felix Lavandier de Curzoñ.

We were to spend several weeks there. Then we would sail for our home in San Domingo, where everything would be in readiness for my reception; for Don Luis had written long letters of instruction to his friends and servants, which were to go direct on the barque *Thetis*, with the new furniture and the stock of goods for the warehouses.

But with all my dreams of this new life, I felt the time to pass slowly with

Don Luis absent. I called my little maid, and had a long, soft evening gown put on, and my hair brushed and coiled. Then my heart grew heavy with loneliness; and when the maid had gone, I knelt on the rug before the fire, and with my head on the cushions of the great chair, I shed the first tears of my new life.

His absence, but for a few hours, left me so desolate and lonely, that I knew then that my happiness was bound up forever in the love, the least look, even, of this man. How painful the silence seemed! My heart throbbed with the least sound in the great house.

Suddenly, I heard his quick step in the long corridor of the hotel. Then, hardly breathing, I sprang up and stood still, till he came and took me in his arms. He kissed my brow and hair.

"Darling, have you been afraid? What, no tea? Why, it's eight o'clock. Ring the bell, Paula petite, and then I must tell you what my old friends said about the new Countess of Villemaceda." And

then we sat down to a dainty supper
before the blazing fire, and I thought
it wonderful that life had ever come to
be, to me, so sweet, so dreamful, so
grand.

The next morning, when the bells
were chiming forth their morning hymns,
we stepped into old Trinity. I love
the grand old church. The chanting
strains of the music I heard there filled
my soul with new thoughts of God and
heaven; and as we passed out, the rolling tones of the organ seemed to breathe
a heavenly benediction on our marriage.
So it seemed to my happy heart, good
Padre.

He was so very tender of me! We
went to Wallack's theatre one evening,
and then carelessly lingered, till all the
cabs and hacks had left the street. So
we walked to our hotel along Broadway
at midnight in the cold, clear moonlight.
But I was happy on the lonely street,
and my New England blood rejoiced
in the walk. But Don Luis was distressed, and blamed himself bitterly for

not having ordered a carriage. When we were home, he wrapped me up, placed me in the big armchair before the fire, and watched me anxiously, while we talked of our departure for Martinique.

The next day the neat little ship *Yarrow* spread her white sails in a stiff breeze, and sped out of New York harbor like a thing of life. As I stood watching my native land fading from my view, Don Luis came and took me by the arm.

"Come below, Paula, child, and see what I have done for you," he said.

Then I found that the cabin had been fitted up especially for me, with all the comforts and luxuries I might need.

There were old authors, new magazines, water-color paints, brandy, fruits, candies, and everything his kind heart could suggest.

It was cold outside, and we sat by the bright fire in the saloon, till a rough sea sent me to bed.

The third day Don Luis wrapped

me in a heavy shawl, and carried me on deck in his strong arms. There I revived in the fresh air; and Captain Benton, a tall, serene-looking man, came and spoke to me gravely a moment. Then he took a small Bible from his pocket, and sat down close to us and read, beginning with the lines, "If I take the . wings of the morning, and dwell in the uttermost parts of the sea, even there shall thy right hand lead me, and thy right hand shall hold me." I looked at Don Luis' face bent over me, and my heart was full of love and of confidence in the future.

When my husband took me below, he laid me on the lounge, and read from Goldsmith. Then I kissed him, and told him I would go on deck alone the next day. And so I did, but Captain Benton met me, and he and Don Luis both cried, "Bravo, bravo, Madame!"

As every day brought us to a warmer climate, we spent much of our time on deck, with the cabin boy to wait on us, to bring our rugs, books, and dainties;

and the captain to read to us his inevitable chapter in the Bible.

As we approached the warmer and smoother seas, the good ship was on her best behavior; there was just breeze enough to keep her steady on her southern course.

In those days we had long, long talks as we walked the deck, when the heat of the day was over. Then there were lazy days, when we read and slept under the awnings over our deck chairs.

We were the only passengers, and it seemed as if the ship, the calm tropic seas, the sea birds, and the distant sails were made only to be a part of my new life of love and rest.

One morning, with a cry of "land," we were able to see the distant hills of Martinique through the mist.

Then the ship lay close to the shore all day off Port de France. Never, while memory lasts, shall I forget those rich purple-blue hills, the heavy green forest trees, the palms against the blue air, and the greens of the beautiful little valley

open to the sea, — all wrapped in that
exquisite misty veil of the tropical islands.

The next day the captain and mate
took us ashore in a row boat, and Don
Luis, without a word to warn me of the
beauty I was to see, took me to walk in
the Savane, the great green public square
of Port de France.

Holding up my white embroidered
gown, I walked into the grand avenue
of tamarinds and palms, as in a dream.
It was a new richly luxuriant world; and
the deep greens of the trees, the heavy
drooping vines, the rank perfumes, the
gay spots of bloom, — all worked together
to call me out of myself, and to place my
mind in a strange state of receptiveness
and imagination.

I walked on bewildered, and all at once
I found myself before that wonderful
white dream, "that creation of a master
sculptor," the marble statue of Josephine.

Seven tall palms stood like self-stationed
guards around her; the figure has a hu-
man charm, and I stood absorbed, looking
up into the sweet life-like face. She wears

D

the robes of the First Empire, her arms and shoulders bare, and one hand leans upon a medallion bearing the profile of Napoleon.

On her head is the crown her lover Emperor placed there, and around her neck is lifted up white, delicate lace worked out in detail. She is looking back, with a quiet plaintive smile, over the purple space of the summer sea to the place of her birth,— the beautiful, sleepy Trois-Isle.

My eyes were filled with tears.

"Sweet, unhappy Josephine!" I murmured. Then letting fall my long white skirt, I sank in the green grass at her feet.

My whole frame trembled. Was it her spirit, dear Padre, that had touched my soul with a sudden, deep impress of pain and fear?

"O Luis!" I cried, and turned to find him. I saw that he was not at my side. He evidently had not come with me to the centre of the Savane.

Then I struggled to my feet and kissed the hem of the marble garment.

I have always loved and pitied the Empress Josephine, whose falling star carried with its fate the Emperor Napoleon and the Empire; so with long enraptured glances backward, I slowly turned away, and sought the tall form of my husband in the wilderness of soft drooping greeneries.

I found him near the entrance, sitting on the pedestal of a statue, his head bowed in his hands.

But he looked up as I came near. He was quite pale.

"I felt suddenly ill," he said. "It is too close and quiet here; let us go back."

So, unmindful that some spirit had touched our hearts in prophecy, we were rowed back over the azure sea to the deck of the *Yarrow*.

Chapter IV

The Tray of Jewels

(The Happiness continued)

THE next day we were bound south, with a fair wind, directly across the Caribbean Sea on our way to the quaint little Dutch island of Curaçoa.

But the wind lulled, and after a few hot, calm days, on a sea of glass, we sighted our port with joyful hearts.

Then darkness overtook us, and we anchored outside for the night.

At daybreak we lifted anchor, and the *Yarrow* slowly made its way up a narrow lagoon, and was moored to a long stone wall, where all the blacks and whites of the little town had crowded to watch our landing.

Don Luis had been, in fact, the merchant prince of Curaçoa, and word had already gone ashore that he was on the ship with an American bride.

With nervous hands I dressed myself in a soft thin black dress, rich with lace, and drooped a wide lace hat over my flushing cheeks. When my husband came down for me, he looked at me with careful scrutiny; then he took my two white hands in his and put them to his lips.

"No one could find any fault with you — no one," he murmured; "you are perfect."

Then he handed me up and across the deck, as if I had been a princess, and I stood facing the motley crowd of men, women, and children, of all classes and colors, who stared at me, yet stood back respectfully as we walked on shore. We at once turned down the wall, by which we came presently to an oddly built picturesque stone mansion close to the wall of the lagoon.

Before we reached the entrance, Don Luis stopped me and said:

"This old Dutch mansion is mine.

Mrs. Morse, a Dutch woman, a widow, once a servant in my family, has charge of it, and will be your hostess; she will try to please you; let them all wait upon you as they will."

When we reached the entrance, there was a large, angular Dutch woman waiting on the broad veranda to receive us; a gayly dressed, light-brown girl stood beside her, and a train of negro servants were crowded against the wall behind.

I was almost swept off my feet by my welcome. In a moment I found myself in a large easy chair by the window of a great shadowy room overlooking the stone wall and the sea.

Don Luis talked in that strange foreign tongue to them all, while the servants crowded around to wait upon me. My gloves, my hat, my veil, and parasol were carried away, each article by a separate servant.

A quaint, heavy Dutch table was brought up, and coffee and meats, oranges and bananas, were served to us.

"This is Felicia, your maid," said Don

Luis, and a handsome young woman, nearly white, was bowing beside me.

"And this is Florencia, who will wait upon you both," and a black girl in a yellow dress came up behind her.

Don Luis went out then to meet his business friends, and to look after his merchandise with which the *Yarrow* was laden, and I was left to be looked at and waited on, for not a word of this strange Dutch jargon could I speak or understand.

So I wrote a note to Captain Benton to send me some books from the cabin, and sent it out by Felicia; then I settled myself in my chair against a cushion that Florencia brought.

A small merchant ship lay against the wall directly under the broad open window, and my attention was immediately attracted to a rather fine-looking young man who lay reading in a deck chair under an awning. Very soon he got up, put on a travelling hat, which added to his jaunty appearance, and walked back and forth, occasionally giving his attention to the bales of goods that were being carried

up from the hold by black porters, and
deposited on the wall. If he gave me
some attention, too, I did not know it,
for he had excellent manners, and kept
his eyes to himself.

And that could not have been easy, for
I was the centre of attention that day in
Curaçoa, and a procession of white, black,
and yellow women and servants was
quietly passing by on the wall to get a
peep at Don Luis' American bride.

I was not alone, for Mrs. Morse and
the servants were going in and out,
ostensibly to wait upon me, but in reality
to look me over, and jabber to each other
about me.

I became conscious slowly that there
was one person in the room who had
not moved since I entered. She stood
in a far dark corner, and her black glittering eyes were fixed steadily on me. She
must have been six feet tall, and very
slim; she looked like a piece of bronze
statuary. She was so very old!

There was a red bandana around her
shoulders and a bright turban on her

head. I noticed that her lips moved,
and when there was a lull in the Dutch
jargon, I knew that she was saying something over and over, and she kept raising
her skinny finger and pointing it at me.
After a while I could distinguish the
words,—they were French and I understood them.

"La femme de Curzoñ! La femme de
Curzoñ!"

She was a weird, witch-like appearing
object. I grew so nervous that I
motioned to Felicia, and pointed to the
corner.

"Sheba! Sheba!" cried Felicia.

"Sheba! Sheba!" cried Mrs. Morse.
Then they led the poor creature from
the room.

As they went out of the room, I was
startled by something coming through
the window and falling in my lap. It
was an apple, a big, rosy, American apple.
I looked out; the little ship had unfurled
its sails and was just turning away from
the wall, and the young man sprang, as
I looked, from the wall to the deck of

the ship. Then he lifted his hat, bowed to me, and disappeared down into the vessel. I knew that it was he who had thrown the apple, and I was so annoyed that I picked it up to throw it back; then I noticed a hole in it and a piece of paper thrust in. In curiosity I drew it out, and read these strange words, —

"Look out for the breakers, little woman. — A friend."

I tore it angrily into bits with burning cheeks.

It was offence enough to have any one be so rude; but an American! He should have known better.

At three o'clock Don Luis came, and, in the midst of what seemed to be the wildest excitement, dinner was served in the room.

First a black girl got a table-cloth from a curious antique set of drawers; another one came running in with napkins; Mrs. Morse unlocked a drawer in the wall and took out some silver; Felicia stood up on a chair, like a pretty figure on a clock, and lifted down a silver fruit dish; Florencia parted a white curtain over a hole in the wall, and took out a great blue platter; and out of half a dozen cubby-holes came all sorts of curious dishes.

But the dinner was worth all the trouble, — fish, meats, green peas, wine, bananas, mangoes, other fruits then new to me, and coffee in the daintiest cups I had ever seen. There was a servant to every dish, and Don Luis sat smiling opposite me and talking gayly to the various members of this free and happy household.

After dinner we were shown to our large, clean, airy room above. Felicia unpacked my trunk, and I sat in a rocker in my long white wrapper, the soft sea air blowing over me, while Felicia brushed my hair, and Don Luis sat near me writing and patiently answering my many questions.

*   *   *   *   *   *

You will forgive me, good Padre, for lingering so long over these happy hours; for, indeed, they were so happy that my heart now is really with them all the time.

That night I moved uneasily in my little white bed, and Don Luis heard me from his couch by the window.

"If you want anything," he said, "call Felicia." In a second Felicia was at my side with a cool glass of lavender water.

"Why, where was she?" I asked in amazement.

"She lies on the rug outside the door," he said. "She is there to wait upon you."

And she lay there every night I was in Curaçoa.

*   *   *   *   *   *

That same night poor old Sheba appeared to me in a dream, pointing her long finger and shrieking out in French,

"La femme de Curzoñ! La femme de Curzoñ, pauvre petite!"

So as soon as we awoke, I asked Don Luis about Sheba.

He told me that she had been his French mother's servant; that she had been his nurse and his son's nurse; that she was now too old to nurse the little Felix.

"And she is very much offended," he

said, " because we do not let her nurse the child. Poor old soul! Don't let her worry you, Pauline."

But I was annoyed, for it was a hideous dream.

While we were having coffee in our room one morning, I said to Don Luis, " Now, when is the best time for me to go shopping?"

" No time," he answered firmly, frowning slightly ; " ladies never shop here."

But ladies might select, and in a few moments four black natives came up to my room laden with boxes of merchandise.

There was everything rich and beautiful a lady might want. I selected some white dresses, slippers, and fans, and then Don Luis, with a wave of his hand, ordered the goods and porters away.

At the eleven-o'clock breakfast I could see that preparations were being made as if to receive some honored guest. Rugs were being laid about, and every black shiny servant was polishing a silver dish.

Then Don Luis told me to dress in

my best; and soon after Felicia came running up-stairs calling, " Felix, Felix."

We looked from the window and saw a handsome young woman coming down the wall, followed by a train of servants, the foremost of whom was carrying a child.

Don Luis took me by the arm, and we went down and met them on the broad veranda.

It was Maria Mercedes de Curzoñ, his son's wife, and Felix, the heir.   Don Luis spoke her name to me; she murmured something in Spanish, and looked at me, opening wide her beautiful, languid eyes.

She wore a long white dress with many stiffly starched skirts, and they rattled and rustled as she bowed slightly, and passed in, leaving the steps crowded with gayly dressed servants of all shades of color.   I followed her, and noted the excitement her advent caused in the house, but I could not talk to her.   So I looked about and said, " Felix ? "

Felix was nowhere to be seen.   Felicia

pointed above, smiling; and noting the
absence of Don Luis I slipped out softly,
and went up-stairs to the open door of our
room.

The beautiful little boy, with his dark
curls floating around his head, was seated
in a great chair, and Don Luis was kneeling at his feet, kissing and petting him
with rapturous fondness.

"My precious boy! My own!" he
was saying in English. "I will love you
first and always — my boy, Felix."

A pain came to my heart, then, good
Father. I am such a child-like little
woman — and love was all I had. I
would have gone to kiss the little Felix,
myself, but the pain of jealousy kept
me back, so I went slowly down the
stairs.

Maria Mercedes was still smiling lan-
guidly, and a servant was fanning her with
a peacock fan.

That same night Don Luis awakened
me; the house was quiet. "Come," he
said. He pushed the sleeping Felicia
from the rug with his foot, and led me

down the high balustraded stairs into the
large living-room. He softly closed the
shutters and pushed the bars that fastened
the doors. He put the lamp in my hand
and kissed my brow solemnly.

"There are things here they do not
know of," he said.

Then he took a drawer out from the
wall, removed an interior panel, and reach-
ing far inside, he slid something with a
rasping sound, and then took out a great
tray and placed it on the table.

Taking the lamp from my hand (which
was a wise precaution against my surprise),
he lifted a velvet spread from the tray,
and the sudden flame of many jewels shot
up before my eyes.

Don Luis encircled me with his arm
and drew me near.

There were diamonds, rubies, emeralds,
and sapphires, all settled in the depth of
rich black velvet. He unwrapped a necklace of pearls from a soft silken bandage.
Heavy gold bracelets and curious brooches
of gold lay piled on each other.

Opals and moonstones overflowed from

an ebony casket.   Serpents of gold with
green eyes writhed over velvet pads.

I stood gasping out my tremulous
wonder and surprise.

" Oh, they are so beautiful!" I cried.

Then my husband lifted my face up to
his.

" They are yours," he whispered.
" Those diamonds you may yet wear in
Paris.   No one else knows of them,—they
are safe here,—and sometimes I may need
to use them.   Never speak of them to
any one."

He covered them carefully.

" Now see if you can replace them."

He guided my hands tenderly, and we
put away the tray, closed the iron door,
and replaced the panel and the drawer;
then he put out the light; and gathering
me in his strong arms, he carried me up
the stairs, touching my forehead once on
the way with a light kiss.

And I wondered then if it was not a
sort of penance he was trying to do, on
account of what he had said to Felix.

x

Chapter V

The Señor Hippolite Lavandier

(The Happiness continued)

ONE day I heard a strange noise at my door, and I motioned to Felicia to open it. There stood Sheba. She swung her tall form into the room, and stood pointing with her long, trembling arm from the window. Felicia took her away, then I turned to the window.

Two men were coming down the wall. They were conspicuous objects, and the negroes at work with the merchandise, and the dark women carrying burdens on their heads, were standing still to look at them. One was tall, and almost majestic in appearance, and his long white beard shone like silver in the sun.

He was dressed as an American would be, save for the gleam of a white sash

about his waist, and the broad hat that
shaded his face from me.   The other was
a fat, rolling Dutchman in a white linen
coat and vest; he waddled along with an
air of reflected greatness, turning up his
eyes with manifest respect to the face of
the tall and graceful gentleman.

"Lavandier!" whispered Felicia beside
me, and in a moment she had out my black
lace dress, and was preparing me to go down.

When I was ready Don Luis came
up and escorted me down the stairs with
careful ceremony, Felicia carrying my
handkerchief and fan and lifting my train
behind me.

Speaking in Spanish, Don Luis presented me to the grandfather of the little
Felix; but to the short man he paid no
attention whatever.

After his bow, and a long sharp look
at me from a pair of piercing eyes, the
tall señor paid no attention to me; but he
turned to my husband, and they talked
quietly in Spanish.   I found my favorite
seat by the window, and the servants
brought coffee and fruits.

The Dutchman sat in the doorway and kept his bleary little eyes fastened on me. After he had finished his coffee, he rose slowly, crossed the room, and whispered in the ear of the Spaniard. This brought me another sharp glance, from those fierce eyes, —and immediately something was said by both of them that angered Don Luis, for he sprang to his feet with a few hot words.

The tall señor immediately rose, bowed to me, and walked out of the room with high dignity, the leering Dutchman rolling behind him.

Don Luis seemed to control himself with an effort; he came and kissed my hand with stately ceremony, then followed them up the wall. The servants, open-mouthed, rushed out on the veranda. Then through the shadowy room I saw something move in the corner. It was Sheba — she had been crouched behind the folds of a heavy curtain. She came out, not pointing her finger, but with clasped hands and bent head she came to my side and loomed over me, her sunken eyes wet with tears.

"Vous êtes très jeune!" she said slowly; "pauvre petite! Vous êtes très jeune! Tout est pour Felix. They will kill you, Lavandier is a devil. Pauvre petite!"

"Sheba, Sheba!" cried Felicia, and the servants, with a torrent of Dutch words, pushed her from the room.

Trembling in every fibre, I made my way up to my room. I understood enough of her French to know that something was wrong, and that the grandfather was my enemy.

Don Luis did not come in till late that evening. "What was wrong?" I asked, at once; "was not the Señor Lavandier pleased with me?" He laughed, I thought, uneasily, and turned to the window.

"Don't be distressed, Pauline," he said; "that fool lawyer, that old Dutchman, made me angry. As if it makes any difference that you are so young. But the quarrel does not concern you. Pay no attention to it."

And so he comforted me. But, often, from my window, I could see the tall form of Lavandier moving with my husband on the street and wall; and Don Luis seemed no more so cheerful and happy.

I knew that he was very busy getting ready to embark for Samaná, so I tried in my heart to excuse him for his long absences, and his troubled and nervous manner when with me.

I found out that others loved him besides myself. The next Sunday we went to visit a hospital where the aged indigents were kept in charge of a priest and a few nuns.

We went into the little chapel just as they were having mass, and when it was over the feeble old people came crowding around Don Luis. They all seemed to know and love him. One old man threw his arms about Don Luis' neck, muttering. A nun quietly took him away, and Don Luis turned to me and said gravely:

"You must forgive him, for the poor man says that I am always remembered in their prayers. I shall need a great many prayers, too, Pauline," he continued sadly.

Then for fear others would fall upon him, we hurried away; but Don Luis walked along silently, with a strange, abstracted manner.

Shortly after we sailed for Samaná on the ship *Alondra*. My maid, Felicia, occupied the cabin with me, and Don Luis gave me his attention hurriedly and at long intervals, as if he might have had many other things to occupy his attention.

And when I learned from Felicia that the Señor Lavandier was on the vessel, I kept my room patiently, awed by the memory of that fierce look from his eagle eyes at Curaçoa.

When the ship entered the bay of Samaná, I came on deck. Don Luis came to me, greeted me kindly, and showed me all the points of interest; but when we made preparations to go ashore, the Señor Lavandier gave all the directions, and I saw no more of my husband.

(The End of the Happiness)

Chapter VI

The Master of Curzoñ

(The Padre's Notes. A Translation)

Samaná, May 1. I was annoyed this morning with Margarite, foolish child! She wants to leave her good home with Madame Conard to become the maid of the Señor Luis de Curzoñ's American wife. Margarite is too pretty to be around the House of Palms or the warehouses. She must stay on the hill with the good Madame Conard, where she will be safe. I told her so. She is so many shades lighter than most of the colored girls, that I will get her a good husband, perhaps a trader, if she minds well. But her little head is full of nonsense about fine furniture and carpets that have been recently brought to the House of Palms, and she showed me designedly a few tears from her soft eyes.

56

"Margarite," I cried angrily. "No, I dare not expose you to the dangers you would meet running about the town on errands for an American woman, who will be ignorant of the ways of this country. No, no, stay where you are." So she went away pouting.

Ah, well! The Holy Mary help me! This is a great care on my soul — these pretty Creole girls of mixed blood, who have no fathers or brothers to protect them.

May 2. The running and calling on the street this morning told me that the *Alondra* had cast anchor in the bay.

With the rest of idlers (I know I am an idler at times) I went out to see the landing, for the captain had told us, when he was last here, that he would bring Don Luis and his American bride from Curaçoa.

Having a good marine glass, I was the first one to know that the first boat, which left the ship's side, contained not the Count of Villemaceda and his bride, but the count and old Lavandier, the grandfather of Felix, the heir.

I was at once disturbed in my mind, for I knew that the old don had no business here except to protect, in some way, the interests of little Felix; his own fortune, also, being largely invested in the mercantile ventures of Don Luis.

Then what I saw next filled me with disgust. The white woman (I cared not then what nationality she claimed) was put down in the boat with two black servants of the ship, and the boxes were being lowered to come in the same boat. I shut up my glass and came back with a sorrowful spirit. No Spanish or French gentleman would treat a wife in that way: she was not a wife, she was a mistress.

The captain of the *Alondra* had been but amusing himself with the story of a new countess who would invite us all to an American tea at the House of Palms. For shame on Don Luis to bring a woman of that kind here! As if we were not already wicked enough.

I went into the church to thank the Holy Virgin that she had helped me to be so firm with Margarite.

Sunday evening. When I came from vespers, I stumbled against a tall form leaning against the wall by my door. I paid no attention to the person, as I prefer to be accosted first by those seeking my aid, either as a Doctor of Medicine or as a Servant of God.

But the person followed me into my office ; and when I had lighted my candle, I looked up in the face of one whom I had once esteemed as a friend, — Luis de Curzoñ, the Count of Villcmaceda.

"Go away, go away, you wretch!" I cried, snapping my fingers angrily in his face. "How dare you come into my presence after what you have done? You, who have held the power of morality to be as great as the power of the church! Away with you!"

"But, good Padre, listen to me," began Don Luis.

"Don't 'good Padre' me," I said, newly angered. "I will have no hypocrisy. You brought that creature here — now take her away. Send her where she belongs, and then we will see if there is any penance that will save your miserable soul."

"Doctor Caccavelli, what can you mean?" he said, grasping my arm.

"Mean!" I cried; "it is noised about the streets by the negroes; the Creoles are making jokes about it; the Señor Lavandier has told it to the American consul."

"What?" he asked wildly.

"That you have brought a degraded American woman here—your mistress."

I did not strike him, but he staggered back into a chair, dropped his head on my table, and grasped its edges with his white, firm hands.

I looked down on him, smothering my wrath. When he lifted his head, I turned away to express my contempt.

"Oh, Father, have pity on me!" he cried; "Lavandier owns me body and soul. He has done all this — I am helpless."

"Have pity on you!" I stormed. "Have pity on you? You, who have brought this woman to the House of Palms, where lived the sainted mother of your son, whose soul was so pure it needed no shriving?"

He then thrust both hands toward my face. "Wait," he pleaded weakly; "I will tell you all."

"I will wait for nothing," I cried. "There is nothing to wait for but the vengeance of God that will surely fall upon you. Lavandier has his own sins to answer for,—they are legion. Don't burden him with yours."

With that I came away to my room to pray God to forgive me, if my anger had been unseemly.

May 6. It is worthy of record that I have seen the little unfortunate woman at the House of Palms. And I know now what she is; but what is the cause of her misery, or what may yet be the depth of it, no one but God himself fully knows.

I was annoyed because they sent Julian Carlos. I have no love for him. He knows too much for a darky, and not enough for a good Spaniard; and with his Carib blood and his handsome face, I know not what race ought to claim him.

He thrust his head into my office early this morning, and said in poor Italian, as if he wanted no one to understand but me, "You're wanted down at the house, Doctor Caccavelli — she's sick." I turned not my face from the cordial I was mixing, but I answered speedily and tartly:

"You may tell your master, the count, that my services are for the poor, and that I cannot leave my duties to run at his call."

He went away, but shortly after his insolent face peered in again.

"Good Padre, they say she's dying; she wants a priest."

By virtue of my sacred office I go where I am called, and snatching my medicine case I hurried down to Curzoñ's house, thinking up my English as I ran.

From the warehouse I took the old familiar path through the palm garden to the hallway of the house. Here I hesitated, but the housekeeper came and led me to the room where the first sainted Señora de Curzoñ had received the last sacrament at my hands. But the stuffed furniture and lace curtains from New York had vastly changed the once sombre apartment.

The housekeeper pointed to a bed, and left me alone with my unpleasant mission.

I looked about me and perceived on the white bed, propped up and around by crimson and blue cushions, the form of a woman fully dressed in black. As I approached, she uncovered her white face, and looked steadily at me with her large, dark eyes. She made no motion as I counted her pulse, but still looked fixedly at my face.

"Wretched creature," I said then in English, "will you tell me the nature of your trouble? What can I do for you?"

At this she raised herself slightly and fell back sighing, —

"Oh, sir," she said, "I fear you can do nothing. I am not a Catholic — I am a Presbyterian. I need a friend. Is there no preacher here?"

"Friend," I cried, "by what right do you expect a friend? One who comes here as the willing mistress of a gentleman can claim no friends. I could pray for an ignorant Creole girl, but not for you."

At this she started up wildly, and fell back with a moan that shook her whole slight frame.

Seeing the weakness of her condition, I gave her a few drops of stimulant from my case, and then she looked up at me most pitifully.

"Oh, sir," she said, "is that what they say? No one has been to see me — that is the reason. Oh, my Heavenly Father, help me! Oh, sir, you have a good face. Believe me, it is not true. In that portfolio on the table there, you will find my certificate; get it; read it." I hastened to examine it; it was genuine. I well knew the signature of Don Luis de Curzoñ.

I struck my forehead angrily. Curzoñ had told me nothing; in my hasty wrath, I had not permitted him to tell me anything: I had been misled by the rumors. I turned to Madame Curzoñ, begged her pardon, and sat down by her to re-examine her pulse.

"Señora," I said, "you are in a sinking

condition.   But you have no disease.
You must have nourishment."   Then
she lifted her little white hands to me so
pleadingly.

"Oh, sir," she said, "you are a priest of
God.   If there is no minister of my own
here, will you not help me? You are
the first one to speak to me in English.
May I not ask you? Will you not tell
me what to do?"

"What to do?"   I asked gravely.
"Where is your husband?"

"Oh, sir," with this she sank back again;
and after I had administered a few drops of
brandy from my case, she whispered faintly,

"They are keeping him away from me.
Oh, why does he not come?"

Thinking that she might be mentally
unsound, I took her trembling little hands
in mine, and holding them firmly I proceeded to question her quietly to deter-
mine, if possible, her exact physical and
mental condition.

I soon won her confidence. Then I
said in my heart:

"That old wolf is doing this; Lavan-

F

dier is hungry for the blood of this lamb. He does not want an heir to share the spoils with the little Felix."

It seems there had been high words and quarrels, in Spanish, on the deck of the *Alondra*. Then, after the landing, Curzoñ had withdrawn himself entirely from her. Her maid had been sent away on the *Alondra*. Don Luis had shown her to her room, had given the servants orders for her comfort, and then turned away without a word. She had thrown herself at his feet in the presence of Lavandier, and begged to know in what way she had offended; but he had only torn her hands away, and told her to go and come as she pleased, but to say no more to him. For two days she had sat at the meals with the two men, but in silence and ignored; then with her heart half-broken she had kept her room, and the food the housekeeper brought she had sent away untasted. As she told me this, I cried out:

"What senseless cruelty! Don Luis de Curzoñ has become heartless! He is not like himself! He is insane!"

"No, no, no!" the little woman exclaimed, rising up and falling back. "No, something holds him. Something keeps him. I love him, and he loved me—I cannot forget that."

"But," I said, "has he made no effort to explain his singular conduct to you?"

Then she looked around nervously at the door and windows of the room, and lowered her voice to a whisper.

"One night," she said, "there was a fight in the hall. First I heard Don Luis' voice calling me softly at the door. Before I could admit him I heard two men running; then I heard angry words, but they were in Spanish, so I could not understand them, but they seemed to be scuffling.

"'Cuidado con ostra,' said the voice of that old man; then they slowly went away, and I was so frightened I dare not say a word to any one or go out of my room."

My heart was moved for the sufferer. She was an American. I am proud to do a service for an American, so I gave her my counsel. I reminded her that she was now the Señora Doña de Curzoñ, Countess of Villemaceda; that by virtue of her certificate she was mistress of that great house and the servants.

I urged her to get up and go about with all the dignity she could command; to walk out on the street; to apply herself to learning a few necessary Spanish words, to receive a call from the American consul's wife, in fact, to live to the outside world as if all was well.

I implored her to be patient, and do as her husband had bidden her; and I led her to hope that in due time her relations with him would be restored. I could only hope so myself — I knew nothing.

Then I rang for the housekeeper and ordered food, and at my command the countess ate obediently. After which I took her own Bible from the table, and laid it reverently beside her. Then pointing to the high heavens from whence comes all help, I came away.

I walked through the palms, unmindful of the glimmering blue of the sea and sky exulting through the branches, and coming to the lower end of the warehouse I walked through the long dark aisles blocked with new goods. I found Don Luis over his accounts at a desk, with Lavandier smoking a vile Dutch pipe beside him.

"Señor," I said, addressing myself to the bowed head of Curzoñ, "it is quite useless to send for Dr. Caccavelli; as a doctor of medicine I cannot administer to a mind diseased."

Curzoñ neither moved nor lifted his head.

Lavandier puffed a moment in silence, and then threw me a hostile glance.

"You would favor me much," he said in Spanish, "if you would hold your tongue. We wanted you to see that she does not die. She is going back to New York."

I well knew that I had no reason to expect civility from this old wolf. I further knew, that as great as were my privileges, as a servant of God, that I had no power over these two men. My best resource was silence, and I passed on.

May 6, evening. I went this afternoon to enlist Henry Conard's sympathy for his country woman, and to request Madame Conard to call upon her. Conard's long residence on these islands had given him a professional manner of indifference to the distresses of strangers ; but Madame's warm Italian blood grew hot as mine.

" Brand her as a woman of immorality, and send her home ? they shall not," she cried.

Consul Conard advised us not to interfere, reminding us that two men held the balance of power.

" Anyway," I said, " let us adopt a course of reason. We should treat her as a lady, till we know otherwise. It is evident that Curzoñ has married without first gaining permission of his lord and master. If this poor woman is repudiated and sent home, it will kill that aged mother, she has spoken of to me. She must stay and fight for her position as a proud Spanish or French woman would do. She must not be so foully wronged. She is the Señora de Curzoñ. She shall remain so."

"God wills it, she shall!" cried Madame Conard. "God bless you, noble Padre. Come, Margarite, do make haste. We will dress now and call on the Countess of Villemaceda."

May 9. Doña Pauline, the Countess, has been to mass with Madame Conard. Her firm bearing indicates that purpose has taken the place of despair. I saw her looking pleadingly at the shrine of the Virgin; may the Holy Mary comfort her.

May 13. After serious reflections, I have to-day advised Don Luis' wife, by a verbal message through Madame Conard, that she should by all means withhold from her aged mother and loving sister in Maine any information of her present mental distress. Providence may yet lift the clouds and make the way fair for this gentle American lady that ill-fortune has cast upon these strange shores.

Chapter VII

The Goddess of Silence

(A Letter)

THE HOUSE OF PALMS,
SAMANÁ, May 14, 18–.

MY BELOVED MOTHER AND SISTER:—
Since leaving Curaçoa, I have not had a
chance to send away mail, but the steamer
Thybe is expected to-morrow, and I will
now write you a long letter.

Such a weak pen as mine can never describe to you the beauties of this famous
island and the quaint surroundings of my
new home; but I must try to tell you a
little of them.

When our ship neared my new home, I
came on deck, and saw before me the far-
famed Bay of Samaná. Don Luis had
spoken of its size and beauty, but it broke
upon me as the loveliest picture I had ever
seen. They say that it is finer even than
any inlet in Cuba.

Along the whole north coast of Samaná
stretch coral reefs that form little groups
of islands called Los Ballaenas, Los Canes,
etc., while the shore curves to the edge of
the sea in abrupt hills, and looming above
these at the point of Cape Cabron is the
peak, Pilon d'Azure, rising two thousand
feet above the sea.

The whole coast appeared, as we approached it in the *Alondra*, as a softly
changing panorama of noble hills, beautiful savannas, bold headlands, and lovely
indentations of the coast line, with a belt
of sand and surf separating the rich green
verdure from the pure ultramarine of the
sea.

In fancy, clothe the sides of this bay
with bold hills from two hundred to two
thousand feet high, from which charming
valleys covered with trees and vegetation
slope gently down to the sea; indent the
shore line with coves, or here and there
small harbors, whose white sands glisten
in the sun, and you will have some idea
of the beautiful bay that Columbus himself named the " Bay of Arrows," as it

was the place, it is said, where the first
blood of the children of the New World
was spilt by those of the Old.

The lifting of the morning mist disclosed all these wonders and beauties, and
long before we anchored I could study
the outlines of the little town of Samaná,
situated close to the sea, at the edge of a
little plain ; its red-tiled roofs, in the midst
of the greeneries, glittered in the sun.

My husband's warehouses face the
street, and back of them lies a great
garden of shady palms and vines, and
this queer, low straggling house, from
which paths run down through the garden
to the sea.   One is a walk latticed all the
way, and at its end is fastened a canopied
boat, which sways dreamily in the water
as the gentle tide comes in.   The Padre
tells me that it was sent by my husband,
from New York, for me.

First I must tell, dear Mother, about
this new friend of mine.   I call him my
friend, though I have not seen him many
times.   He's a Catholic priest, but he is
a Christian, a real Christian, — I know

that.   You see, I was ill a few days after
I came (just a little bit sick, do not worry,
dear Mother), and they sent for him.   He
is the priest and physician, too, Doctor Caccavelli ; his other name and title is Marc
Aurèle, Curate of Samaná.

I felt better as soon as I opened my
eyes and saw him.   He is tall, and moves
with a graceful dignity so like my noble
father.   He has a strong yet kind face,
and when he stepped into my room in
his long black cassock and pointed cap,
the power of his presence strengthened
the very air around me.   He speaks
French, Spanish, Italian, and English
fairly well.   He is an Italian by birth
and seventy years old.   His emotions
are pure and natural as those of a child,
and he is so very kind and good!   Do
not worry about me, dear Mother; if
anything should go wrong, this kind
old Father will help me.   God bless
him !

Soon after my arrival Madame Adele
Conard, the American consul's wife, called
upon me.   The next day she sent down

her servant, Margarite, who helped me to dress, and, attended also by an untrained servant from this house, I went to return the call.

The Conards, I think, are going to be good friends to me in this land of strangers.

Mr. Conard, the consul, comes from a fine family of Pennsylvania. He is very quiet and says little, but he seems to have excellent judgment. He already shows a kindly interest in me, and has asked me many questions about my home and people.

He has been consul in different parts of these islands for many years, and Madame Conard says, in her warm way, that she would be heart-broken if the American flag did not wave over her residence.

She is of Italian parentage, but was born in Kentucky and educated everywhere, I should judge. She speaks French, Spanish, and island patois; and her English, when she is excited, is a mixture of all. She plays, sings, and dances like a girl. She has a warm, enthusiastic nature, and the Padre says that all the islanders love her.

She lives on a pleasant little hill overlooking the sea. I can see her cottage from the garden; she calls it the " Adela Villa." She has some American fruit trees around the cottage, which I can distinguish by their soft greens above the dark colors of the tropical trees mingled with them.

Madame Conard either calls on me every day, or sends Margarite with a note requesting me to call on her.

This house of Don Luis' is called the " House of Palms," and it is so surrounded by palms, that I cannot see any other house but the Adela Villa from the windows, — but I have glorious glimpses of the azure sea.

The blacks and natives here speak an island patois, a barbaric mixture of Spanish, French, and everything else.

I think I can soon learn to speak a little Spanish, so that the servants can tell what I wish, anyway. The government of this island is Republican in form, but the ruling classes are Spanish; and Mr.

Conard says that one can never tell just what laws and customs are going to prevail, whether Spanish or French.

Don Luis has a clerk in the warehouse, who is also a sort of official attendant on himself. He has brought the man in to wait upon him at dinner occasionally, and I was led to notice him several times, particularly, both on account of his personal appearance, and good English, and for the reason of the relation of confidence which seems to exist between this person and the Señor Lavandier.

The Padre tells me that he is a native of the island of Trinidad. He says the natives of that island are all handsome. They are a mixture of French and negro, with a hint of Carib blood; they have shapely, slender figures and fine straight profiles. Julian Carlos, this person I speak of, has such a profile and figure, but his skin is a clear yellow, almost white. His hair is a mass of fine glossy curls, in color, a sort of a blue black; he has brown eyes and long silky lashes — and with one glance from under them

he seems to catch Don Luis' slightest
desire.   And he waits upon him about as
one friend would wait upon another.   He
has the manners of an affected Frenchman,
the assurance of a darky; the indolence,
when not under orders, of the Spanish
Creole, and the quickness and adaptability
of an American youth.   He is wonderfully handsome; he calls himself a Frenchman.

*   *   *   *   *   *

I know you are wondering, dear Mother,
how I spend my time.   Madame Conard
says it makes no difference how one
spends the time in this balmy climate.
The window of my room looks down to
the sea, and here I sit much of the time,
the shutter thrown wide open to let in the
flower-scented air.

I have no cares — I could not talk to
the housekeeper, even if she needed my
orders; she goes on just as if I were not
here.   Don Luis told me at Curaçoa,
that I was to do nothing at all at Samaná,
and I suppose that is the way it is to be.

A little colored girl, named Julia, has

been set aside for my service. She knows nothing at all, but I let her sit in the corner and stare at me.

There she sits now while I write. Outside a tropic shower has come up; I hear the rain pattering on the palm leaves, and the water has spattered from the window frame on my paper; but I shall not close the sash — these sudden showers are so sweet and refreshing here.

When I have finished my letter, I will send Julia with it to the house of the American consul, who will send it to the steamer for me; I shall go to work on my picture.

Brides do not often paint pictures, but that is what I am doing. The day after I called on the Conards, they called on me, and I was summoned to receive them in the quaint, oddly furnished dark parlor that I have already named the " Black Room," — it is so sombre and cheerless.

The Conards brought with them several Spanish gentlemen, who addressed me as " Señora La Condesa," in mellow voices, and then sat with a great deal of pleading expectancy in their bright eyes, while the Conards explained their errand.

They had brought with them a canvas taller than I am.

They were Masons, and they wanted me to paint them a picture of the Goddess of Silence for their new hall. These people here seem to think an educated American woman can do anything.

At first I looked at Mrs. Conard and laughed and shook my head. "I know nothing of a Goddess of Silence," I said.

But the lustrous-eyed Spaniards looked so disappointed at this that I began to consider it seriously. Madame Conard came and took my hand, and warmly advised me to paint the picture, if I could.

"It will bring you many friends," she said. "And the Masons are worth having for friends. Do not hesitate, dear little Madame."

So I told them to leave the canvas, and then I went up to the Adela Villa to look over a pile of Masonic books and papers in Mr. Conard's library, where I

G

finally found a rude engraving of the Goddess of Silence.

As soon as I began to work on the picture, the housekeeper and the other servants began to crowd around my door. In order to preserve the privacy of my room, I carried my work to the Black Room, where I am quite willing to have visitors. It is a large square room with mahogany floor and black wainscoting.

The furniture is old and colorless. But I opened wide one of the barred shutters, and this makes a bright corner for me to work in.

Here I am the object of the most unrestrained curiosity.

Don Luis' servants, and some others of the same class of natives, are hovering around the door and the open window much of the time.

And I do not object — it is company for me.

Julian Carlos manifests great interest; he comes in several times a day to see the progress of my work; but I do not talk to him — Madame Conard says he is only a servant.

My Goddess is a beautiful woman, with deep sad eyes and a world of thought in her expression. She has her fingers on her lips, and her lips are so intense with a language of pain and sorrow, that they seem to tremble under her finger; her brow is queenly, and her whole white-robed figure is expressive of patience and strength of purpose.

My own heart trembles as I work, and my brush moves in a strange sympathy with my theme.

Love, as well as Charity, worships the Goddess of Silence, and God only knows what love is, that is silent over all sorrows for love's sake. The Goddess has a look of repose and power. Silence is strong to bring back love that, but for her, would flee away forever.

Sweet and wonderful Goddess! I worship her as I paint, while the sunlight comes and goes, and the warm showers dash down on the palms outside.

Adios, my mother and sister, you shall hear from me often.

PAULA.

Chapter VIII

Five Hundred Pesos for the Countess

(The Padre's Notes)

May 15. I must make a note now of my new entanglement in the affairs of this Señora Doña de Curzoñ, for I may some time be called to account for what I might have done, or what I did not do, for this pretty, innocent American woman.

Yesterday evening I took a long walk through the woods to see Madame Carter, an unfortunate native woman who is married to an American, who gives love, but, alas, not much else except a dismal home in the woods.

Carter is a heretic, yet I must needs carry medicine to his sick wife, and I baptize the little ones in the faith: that is the best I can do for her.

I came to the town while the moon was

yet high and bright, and my way led me along the south enclosure of the House of Palms. I was suddenly arrested by Don Luis, who stepped out from a little gate in the hedge, and laid his hand on my shoulder, in his old familiar way.

"Ah, Padre," he said, in his easy Spanish, "you walk slowly; you are tired. Come into my den. It is not often you favor me any more. I have some new books that I want you to condemn: if you like them, I will not read them. Come in and rest."

This was Don Luis of old, full of fearless cynicism, but a *bon vivant*, a gentleman, and a royal good companion.

He held open the little wicket, and fairly drew me in with a graceful magnetic gesture I could not resist.

The library, which Don Luis called his den, is the end room on the south wing of the house, and accessible, in a regular way, only from his own private apartments. But at the south end is a window opening, almost as large as a door and protected by iron shutters.

We entered through these shutters, and I found the library just as it used to be,—packed with books to the ceiling, its cabinets filled with scientific specimens and grotesque curios.

A lounge and an easy chair were drawn to the centre of the room, and tables crowded with French and English papers and magazines, and books, yet unwrapped, were placed irregularly about.

An American lamp stood unlighted on the table, but six or seven candles were burning in different parts of the room.

I sank into the easy chair, and Don Luis poured out a glass of wine, such as could be found nowhere on the island save in that room.

"There, Dr. Caccavelli," he said, "doff your cap and rest."

He set out a plate of biscuits and some delicate pressed figs, and placed a new book under my eyes. "That's 'Ecce Deus,' a thing I picked up in New York. What do you think of it?"

I ran over the book and shook my head. It was useless to bring up old discussions: we had gone over the ground before.

"Thank you, Caccavelli," he retorted cheerfully from his easy posture on the lounge; "I'll read the book. There's a neat little thing called 'Spading for Life,' about an American who came down here in the tropics and made himself rich raising vegetables, and cured himself of consumption at the same time. I suppose you'll like that."

I did like the book and said so.

"That will do, Doctor, you may take it home," he said, lighting a cigar; "I won't read it. I don't care for people who work. By the way, Caccavelli, I see you are interested in the Señora de Curzoñ and disposed to be helpful to her. I'd like to know what kind of advice you are giving her. It seems to me your policy is rather weak. Why don't you put a stiffer front on things, if you want to help her?"

It sounded like a reproof, but his manners and looks were friendly.

"I beg your patience, Don Luis," I

replied. "I am interested in nothing. I was asked to see that she did not die, and I don't intend she shall. I will give her cordial, and encouragement as well." He laid down his cigar and bent towards me.

"Can't you teach her to fight a little, Padre. She ought to hold her head up and stand her ground. There is no other way. I can't do anything — you see, I am bound hand and foot. If she would only take a certain course, and wait patiently —"

"Wait patiently!" I cried. "What does she know about policy, and what has she to wait for? What did you marry her for? Why did you bring her here, poor little one!"

Don Luis fell back with a deep sigh, and threw out his head pleadingly.

"Why, you see, Padre," he said, "I fell in love with the pretty little gray dove, and I married her with every honorable intention. I did not dream of the fuss Lavandier would make, and the infernal — excuse me, Padre — complications that would

come out of it.   I'll tell you about it, Caccavelli.   It makes no difference, you may
as well know it.   You know I came to
this country — well, rather more gentlemanly and religious than I am now,
but penniless.   My ambition was to make
money, and I did with the help of Lavandier.   The first Madame Curzoñ was his
cousin.   The death of my wife and son
left Felix the only heir on both sides
of the house.   Then my father died in
Spain, and left me his estate and a title,
to which Felix is also the heir.   But it
is encumbered, of course, and Lavandier
would give every peca of his money, and
every drop of blood in his veins, to keep
my family estate and title for his grand-
son.

"About the time of Madame's death,
I had reverses, and Lavandier threw his
entire fortune into the vortex.   All the
property I have, both at Curaçoa and here,
is virtually his, but controlled in my
name.   If I had come down from New
York with some ancient dame, all would
have gone well.   But Lavandier and his

lawyer announced to me at Curaçoa that
there should be no more heirs, and the
old man is here to see that his commands
are obeyed. He wants to wear her out,
to make her give up, and go away. His
first insult was to send our servants back
on the vessel that brought us, and land
her in that ignoble manner with the
luggage."

He paused and dropped into French,
as he always does when excited.

"How can I explain to her?—I cannot
see her alone. My master keeps a spy
at my heels. I cannot explain to her.
Americans cannot understand. It would
seem like cruel selfishness to her—it
would break her heart. It would be
far better to send her home than to let
her stay here in a situation she cannot
comprehend." Then I interrupted him
impatiently.

"There is only one thing you can do,—
take her to your arms, and give her the
love she has the right to expect. What
is property beside her? Let the estate
and title, Felix and all, sink into the sea."

Then he leaned to me, pale but self-controlled.

"If I take her in my arms, dear little pearl of love that she is, — Lavandier would soon find a way, — er, you know! We would be compelled to bury the sweet little heretic in foreign, unconsecrated ground. No, no, let it go on awhile. Let her hold her position; let her make friends. She is mistress of my house; but she must not weep when she meets me accidentally, and break out with imploring words. Tell her to wait and be patient. I can say as Napoleon said, 'My destiny is more powerful than my will.' Tell her I said that, will you? Lavandier cannot live always, and then I will be guardian of Felix and the master of everything. Do you think she will understand, Padre?"

I shook my head; I told him that I feared she would not. American women want love and companionship: their ideas on other subjects are not politic. But I thanked him for his confidence, and assured him that I would be kind to her,

although I felt contempt for his weakness
— and I told him so.

"My good Caccavelli," he said, "it is
not weakness, it is my iron destiny —
have some consideration, won't you?"

Then he pressed upon me another glass
of wine, and walked with me to the wicket
gate. As I went away, I thought I saw
him fall prone in the grass in the darkness, but I did not stay nor pity him.

＊　　＊　　＊　　＊　　＊　　＊

May 16. This morning while I was
thinking over this conversation of last
evening, I remembered that the steamer
Thybe was due from San Domingo on its
way to New York, and I thought it advisable to go down to the House of Palms
to see if the Señor Lavandier would make
any attempt to send the Señora de Curzoñ
away. I am not afraid of the old arch-
plotter, and I felt it to be my duty to
prevent any such precipitous occurrence.

Such an event could never be properly
explained in the señora's own country;
her position there would be forever com-
promised, and the disgrace would surely

bring that proud New England mother to her grave.

As I passed through the palms I met Julian Carlos standing in my way, looking as nonchalant as if he owned the island, and had nothing to do but to look at it. I knew he was there awaiting some orders, and that his master must be close by.

The wide hall door stood open, and led by the odor of the Dutch pipe, I went straight to the great salon on the northeast corner of the house, a gloomy apartment, that the señora has already named the "Black Room."

It was just as I expected — Lavandier was there, and he held the throne of power, seated, legs crossed, in a high-back chair by the antique centre table. The countess was standing by her picture, clinging to a chair back. She wore a long black dress, that made her look like a reed; she was pale, but her mouth had a firm look, and her dark eyes were snapping as if some ancestral English blood had flashed up in her veins to aid her in her great extremity.

Don Luis was pacing restlessly back and forth on the other side of the room.

The countess started to approach me as I entered; but, at a significant motion from Lavandier, she stepped back.

The men gave me no heed, and I remained standing by the door.

The Señor Lavandier went on speaking in a guttural manner in Spanish to Don Luis. Finally, he emphasized his remarks by a sharp rap on the table.

Julian came in, as if it had been a signal, and deposited a bag of money on the table.

"Very well," said Lavandier to him in Spanish, "count out five hundred pesos for the countess. Matters of urgent necessity call her to New York. She takes passage on the *Thybe* to-day."

Don Luis stopped walking; Julian untied the bag, and in a slow, aggravating manner of importance began to clink out and stack up the money on the hard, heavy table.

The countess grew a shade paler, and threw a long glance of appeal to me.

Don Luis came forward almost to her; he was haggard and white, as if he had spent a sleepless night.

"Oh, I beg of you, Pauline," he said in English, "do as I have said: go home, go away for a while. I cannot, dare not, tell you what miseries await you here. Pauline, my child, pity me, forgive me, and go away."

Then the little lady straightened up, and folded her hands on her breast, and her whole attitude was a passionate prayer.

"Oh, Don Luis," she said softly, "you loved me once — you love me now — I will dare everything for you — I cannot go."

Then her voice fell so low I could not hear what she said.

But Don Luis turned away, swaying like a tall tree in the wind. I saw that he was ill. I was at his side immediately, and I placed my arm around him and led him to a sofa in the corner.

He was speechless; he tried to motion me away with an imploring gesture; but I bent over him, shielding him with my gown.

I thrust my hand to his side. What I then discovered I will not record even here. It is his secret and mine. I administered a few drops of tonic, and stood quietly by him, shielding him and holding his wrist.

The pesos were still clinking suspiciously on the table, and Lavandier was tying up the bag. Then Julian took the money, and with his most obsequious bow handed it to the countess, who still stood in her corner affrighted, yet defiant.

For an instant she stood like a statue holding out the tray; then, all at once, she flung it contemptuously. The money fell in a shower, and the tray went spinning to the floor.

"I defy you all," she cried; "I shall not go. I shall stay for my rights, and I will have them."

Lavandier quietly stood up in grave surprise. He comprehended the hostility — that was all. Then he turned to me.

"Good Padre," he said in Spanish, "I am glad you happened in. Will you inform the lady that we don't want her here any more?

"Julian, will you tell Madame Grand, the housekeeper, to have her trunks sent out?"

Then I walked forward, and my gesture was such that the insolent Julian shrank away, and Lavandier looked startled. Then I speedily brought a finish to this prolonged insult to the American lady.

"There will be no trunks brought out," I said; "you cannot do this thing, Lavandier, Señora de Curzoñ is a wife. She cannot be divorced. The laws of this island give her an establishment and a support, separate, if she wills, but not a divorce. You cannot send her away — you are trying to frighten her away. You have failed. I beg you to go out and leave her in peace."

The old dog had grown tired enough of the scene by this time. He never makes a prolonged open fight. He looked at me quite civilly for a moment, then he walked over and took Don Luis by the arm, and the two went out.

H

Julian took the bag of money, and he would have gathered up the loose coins, but I stood over them with my gown, as if I had no intention of moving. So he slunk out, and I collected the coins and carried them over to the countess, who was sobbing in her chair.

She shook her head at the coins, but she knelt at my feet and kissed my gown, and thanked me over and over for what I had done — which was nothing, nothing at all.

The money I brought away with me. I will keep it for her, she will need it. Lavandier made one step too far. He gave it to her, and he cannot recall it.

Chapter IX

The Canopied Boat

(A Letter)

THE HOUSE OF PALMS,
SAMANÁ, June 20, 18–.

MY DEAR SISTER NELL:—Amid the
glory of the June showers and sunshine,
I draw my little satinwood desk up to my
open window to begin my letter to you,
as I learned from Madame Conard that a
steamer bound for New York will call
here about the twenty-seventh of this
month.

I wish you could know how lovely,
how incomparably sweet, is this tropic
June! One minute the sun shines broad
and hot on a little sand plat outside my
window, and a gay bird, mute as my Goddess of Silence, perches there a moment
with quivering wing; then, suddenly, a

99

shadow sweeps my room, and great rain-drops come flying in, while the bird flashes past my casement.

Then the rapid growth of the vegetation is a fascinating study.

I know it was but two weeks ago that Don Luis went through the grounds with several laborers and ordered all the weeds and undergrowth removed. To-day there is a new mat of growth everywhere; the wild vines, gay with blossoms, have covered the rose bush under my window, and are ready to climb into my room.

I seldom go out to eleven o'clock breakfast, for many reasons, but Madame Grand, the Spanish-speaking Dominican housekeeper, sends me always a satisfactory luncheon by my maid Julia.

This morning she sent me an arapa (a cake of green corn and cocoanut), an omelet, delicate coffee, fried bananas, and mangoes.

The repast was served on some quaint silver dishes that Margarite looks upon with great awe; she says they came from

France, and were the property of Don Luis' mother.

Margarite is a great help to me; Madame Conard allows me part of her time, for a slight consideration, while Julia is in training. Margarite speaks a little English, but I think Julia will never learn it; however, she brushes my hair nicely, and Madame Grand is teaching her how to take care of my clothes.

For errands she always goes for Margarite, and the two go out together.

When Madame Conard and I go out, we are always followed by the two servants. As an American lady, I am the object of much curiosity; yet the most noble of all the Countesses of Villemaceda, in her château, could not have been treated with greater courtesy and respect, by all classes, than I am, in this Spanish republic.

The Padre tells me that the Spanish people of family are very quick to notice the marks of genuineness and good breeding in strangers, and people are rated, generally, for what they are.

Since I wrote you last, I asked the kind old curate to write you. I knew his French would be perfectly intelligible to you, and not to others who might chance to see the letter. I asked him to tell you, for me, that my position here was being rendered somewhat unpleasant by the opposition to me of the Señor Lavandier, the grandfather of the heir Felix. I asked him to assure you that I was perfectly safe, and secure in my position in my own household, that I was brave, and did not shrink before this unexpected hostility. I felt you would be less shocked to hear of it in this way, and to know from such good authority, that I was really getting along very nicely.

My husband, Don Luis, fears the Señor Lavandier, and thinks it best to humor him somewhat; yet he is perfectly considerate of my position and all my comforts.

Yesterday, when I was painting on my Goddess of Silence, I looked up and saw that all the servants of the establishment had crowded into the room, headed by the self-important Julian Carlos, who was rudely mimicking my motions.

I arose, greatly annoyed; just at that moment Don Luis and Lavandier chanced to come into the hall.   Don Luis is so gentlemanly, I did not think he could be angry, but he certainly was then.   He strode into the room and hurled the surprised darkies right and left, reproving them sharply in Spanish.

Then he turned to Julian in English. "Get out of here, you insolent ape!" he said; "I'll teach you to treat my wife in this way! Don't apologize, you rascal, — go on!"   Then he turned to me:

"Pauline, I am sorry; this will not occur again.   These servants shall treat you with respect, even if I do not."   He was very pale, he hesitated, and was on the point of taking my hands, when Lavandier walked directly to us and led him away.

I thought that he was ill; but I dared not interfere with the fierce-looking old don.

*   *   *   *   *   *

June 22. Madame Conard (I call her
Adela now, we are such good friends)
came down yesterday afternoon, saying,
as she entered the room, —

"A walk, let us have a walk, Doña
Pauline; you have not yet seen the
forest, — the forest will charm you so
much!"

She kissed me effusively.

"See," she said, "you are wearing
your soul out painting the Silent Goddess; the color of your cheeks is going
away."

So, after we had had coffee and fruit in
my room, we started out.

Madame Conard wore a green silk
dress, walking length, a small mantilla
draped around her head, and she carried
a large lace-draped parasol. I wore my
drooping lace hat and my white linen
walking suit. Our maids wore coarse
white dresses, made with a sort of blouse
waist and short sleeves.

Their heads were wrapped with gay
bandanas, and Margarite wore shoes, but
Julia did not.

We went out through a curious gate in a stone wall on the east side of the grounds, and took a path through the shrubbery toward the woods.

I think I began to notice, for the first time here, the deep, rich tones of the landscape.

I experienced a sense of exultation in the charms of my surroundings, and I felt a gladness all through my being that I could live among such overflowing luxuries of nature.

I began to sing little snatches of song, and Adela cried from the path before me, "Ah, the dear little countess is happy now! I am glad."

We walked on, through the tangles, and presently were passing into a belt of limes, pomegranates, and coffee trees, — the neglected fringe of some old Spanish plantation. I could see the dancing blue sea in broken glimpses through the openings, and the love of life and pleasure that is my real nature began to dance in my heart: I felt that I could be happy in a measure here, whatever should happen.

We could see the dark wall of the forest looming up beyond, and when I saw that Madame Conard was going straight on, I stopped and called — "Mia Adela, are you going to the forest? Oh, do not. I am afraid!"

"It is only a little way," she answered; "come on, nothing shall harm you, my child."

But I was almost afraid at first to enter that deep, dark ocean of drooping limbs and heavy clinging vines. I could not distinguish one tree from another — they were pressed so closely together overhead, and literally tied with the ropes of twining vines.

It was a weird place — there was something awful and overpowering in the scene. I stood still to look up into the blackness above, searching for the far-distant violet of the rare gaps in the foliage. I was absorbed; I had forgotten where I was, when suddenly a rich voice spoke,

"Your pardon, Señora."

Some one was arrested by my presence in the narrow path.

Then I was looking into the face of a tall gentleman, a wonderfully handsome man, who was smiling a little at my surprise.

I know I flushed scarlet, as I moved one side. He bowed gracefully and passed on.

My friend Adela was waiting, and she was much amused at my adventure.

"It is Don Juan Portola," she said, "a very grand señor,— a Cuban gentleman. He comes here sometimes. We are on his estate, and this great mahogany and satinwood forest is his.

"Ah, mi vida, but is he not handsome, Doña Pauline? Such eyes! Ah, it is a sad pity you are married, my love!"

Then she immediately forgot the incident and her trivial remarks, — and went on, — but I shall not forget about it.

Our path soon brought us to an opening, and Madame Conard stopped, all smiles, and caught my arm.

"This is what I have brought you to see," she said — "the home of an old Kentucky negro, who speaks your language. It is old Uncle Williams and his wife Susanna. They will be so glad, so happy to see you — it will make you laugh, dear child."

I saw several low-thatched huts, with woven sides (palencas), surrounded by palm trees, and calabaza (pumpkin) vines were running riot all about them.

"Wait," said Adela; and she sent Margarite on to announce our coming. The two old colored people came out with uplifted hands, and we went forward, through a row of hollyhocks, to the door of the largest palenca. My surprise was not equal to my pleasure. It was like seeing old "Uncle Tom" himself. Such a clapping of hands and shouting of "Bress de Lord!"

"Thank de Lord that my eyes am come to see a real white lady once more," cried the old man.

At this Adela made a wry face, as if she thought they might have considered her a lady, and we went into the palenca, where we were offered ginger wine and watermelon, while the old man brought out his banjo, and Adela's eyes sparkled, while he strummed some old plantation tunes. These old darkies are devout Methodists. They can read, but only the Bible and their hymns.

They were freed by a kind master before the war, and were sent out here — they still live with the memories of their youth.

Madame Conard was truly wise and politic to take me out to show me this genuine bit of "old Kentucky" among the palms. It was refreshing. I have been smiling over it ever since.

And Aunt Susanna's "Come once mo', honey, don't you be long," is still ringing in my ears.

* * * * * *

June 25. It is very warm to-day, and there have been no sweet showers to cool the air. I am relaxed, and so weary from the unusual excitement of yesterday, that I have had to keep my room all day. But I must add to my letter an account of it for you, as a steamer is due in a few days.

Yesterday was St. John's day, and my picture of the Goddess of Silence has gone to its place in the new Masonic hall. Mr. Conard, with several other Masons, came for it in the morning, and I was well paid for my labor by the pleased expressions that shone on the faces of the Spanish gentlemen, and with the warm "gracias, gracias, Señora," with which they bowed themselves out.

I had five different invitations, all in Spanish, to come to the dedication ceremonies. The new hall is on the bay, west of Samaná; it is best reached by a short row on the bay. So the Conards came down for me, and we went in my boat.

I told you about my canopied boat, did I not?

When I came out into the hall, dressed in my black lace gown, the American consul said gravely, "Don Luis ought to go."

Inspired with new courage, I took Madame Conard's arm, and we walked into the drawing-room where my husband and Lavandier were having their eleven

o'clock breakfast.   I bowed with my best
dignity to Lavandier, then formally asked
Don Luis if he would not like to ac-
company us.

To our surprise he laid down his cigar,
and said it would give him great pleasure.

We immediately passed out, leaving the
old man, who dared not show hostility
before Madame Conard, frowning like a
storm cloud.   Mr. Conard joined us in
the great hall; Don Luis sent Julian
for another servant to row, and we four,
with the two servants, went down to the
latticed walk to my boat.   Don Luis
handed in Madame, I stepped in with
the American consul, and we were rowed
off dexterously and quickly.

It was all done impulsively, and there
I was out on that exquisite summer sea,
facing my unhappy husband, who has
separated himself from me because his
fear of another is greater than his love
for his young wife.

Madame Conard was highly excited, and
talked constantly in her bright charming
way; but I did not hear her.

I looked past Don Luis' pale face, to
the palm-fringed shore, the dainty little
islands, the boat loads of people passing
along with us, and lived a month of dreams
in those few moments.

Don Luis was bending slightly towards
me, with a look of mingled admiration and
sorrow.

Suddenly he straightened up and began
speaking to Mr. Conard.

He said he was not a Mason and was
not interested in the dedication ceremonies, and that if we would excuse him, he
would return with the boat, and send it
for our use later.

So, when we landed, he handed me out,
held my hand a moment, and then he was
gone, and Julian Carlos was leaning over
his flying oars and smiling insolently.

I was so dazed, and so filled with a
strange tremor, that the rest of the afternoon seemed to me like a dream. The
Master of the Lodge came and escorted
me to the hall. I saw that they were
trying to show me great honor and attention, on account of my picture of the

Goddess of Silence that looked down upon me so pitifully from the wall.

All the best people in Samaná were there, and the event was evidently one of great interest to them; but all the doings of the grand señors with the books, and the smiles of the soft-eyed señoras in the audience, seemed to me only like some old dim picture, for the sorrow of my heart was choking up and crowding out all else.

I remember being thanked again by a group of officers, but before it was over I begged the Conards to take me back to my boat, which had come with two lithe handsome Creole rowers.

I newly love my pretty boat now. (It is so very pretty — the seats are upholstered and the canopy lined with pink silk.)

The two young men shot it over the glassy waves like an arrow.

Madame Conard was delighted with the day, and when we parted in the palm garden, she embraced me and whispered,

" All will be well, my love, — I know, — have courage ! "

1

But I have no courage. Yes, I ought to have, I will not talk that way. Don Luis will surely set aside this difficulty in good time, and bring back the happy days I spent on the *Yarrow*, and in that quaint stone mansion at Curaçoa.

Chapter X

The Lost Cloak

(A Letter continued)

June 26. It is yet another day before
the steamer comes, and I will try and
finish this letter, my dear sister, to tell
you of my experience of last evening. It
is next to having you with me to sit and
write you about these strange occurrences,
and I know you will tell mother only
what you think advisable, for I do not
want her to be overtroubled about this
unfortunate daughter, so far away from
her own country and people.

Last evening, after our formal and
silent dinner in the dining-room, I went
out on the little balcony that adjoins my
room and settled myself in my hammock.
It was not yet dark, and I had several
of your letters, looking over them for
company.

As the light began to fade under the palms, I was moved with a girlish longing to go out and walk, as free as if I were in a New England town, and alone with my thoughts and nature.

Nature is so incomprehensibly lovely to me here.

I wanted to see her by night and under the bright stars, that were so near and sweet to me over the deck of the *Yarrow*.

I was dreaming how enjoyable such a thing would be, when I heard a footstep behind me, a soft voice I have learned to love, and Madame Conard's warm arms were about me.

"Oh, Doña Pauline," she said, "we want you to go. We must have you, — I cannot go without you. Come, come, get yourself ready!"

"Go!" I cried, "I shall be delighted. Where?"

"To see poor Madame Carter," she said hurriedly; "she is very sick, and one of her little ones is dying. She is alone, there is no woman with her. The Padre is going, — he says I must go too, — I have a knowledge of such things, you see, I can help; but I will not go without you. Come, come, Doña Pauline, the Padre waits."

I had time only to catch my long round cloak, and the dainty pink fascinator you sent me, when she hurried me off.

"Where do we have to go?" I said, as we went through the gate in the stone wall. The Padre was walking ahead of us and moving rapidly in his quick, nervous way.

"It is out there where Uncle Williams lives, a little further down to the sea. There is an old sugar mill there, long abandoned, desolate. Carter is only poor white trash, I think, to live there. It is not as good as Aunt Susanna's palenca."

She walked on to keep up with the Padre, and I followed, not caring where, only delighted that something had happened to grant me my wish.

These tropical nights have a splendor you cannot imagine.

Your Northern eyes will never comprehend till you come and see it. The sky is so near, that it seems a part of the earth; and the stars glitter down, larger and brighter than they do in the north. The moon seems twice as large, and it swings out in the sky with a fascinating magnetism. I kept looking at it, and stumbled along after Adela till she came and took my hand to force me to keep up with her. At the entrance of the forest, the Padre waited for us, and then we proceeded on silently, through the weird darkness of that mysterious place. After passing Uncle Williams' palencas, it was perhaps but a quarter of a mile to our destination, which was a wreck of a place right down by the sea.

You will not wish me to describe to you the tumble-down old sugar mill; but there was a nice opening here, and we could look out over the bay, and could discern some of the houses in Samaná.

The Padre took us into a big barn of a place, partly divested of sidings. In one corner a rickety pair of stairs led to a loft-like floor above. I blushed for America, when I found this American family living in one corner of this loft. There were no partitions, and the comforts were very crude.

We found the poor little child dead: Adela and I laid it out on a table, and the priest lit a candle at its head and said some Latin prayers.

Then the Padre told me I had better go below to wait; so I crept down the stairs and went out in the moonlight to listen to the soft murmurs of the waves on the smooth shore, and watch the bits of silver sparkles dancing on the water under the moon.

There was a merchant ship anchored, not very far away, and as I stood looking out a canopied boat came from the direction of Samaná, stopped at the ship awhile, and then came slowly towards me, as if to make a landing.

There were two men in the boat, and as I did not want to meet strangers, I went in and started to climb the stairs. Adela came down and stopped me. "Don't come up," she said, "it isn't over yet. You are tired waiting, my child. Ah, this is what

you can do, dearie ; go back and stay with
Aunt Susanna till we come. It is such a
little way, you can't lose the path."

That plan suited me very well, so I
went out. The boat was quite close then.
It looked like my own pretty little canopied boat, and events proved that it
really was. I hurried on to my path,
which was through an open thicket here
— I could see all about me. I had gone
about half way, when I heard a slight
noise. I looked around and saw that two
men were following me. I gave a little
scream and began to run. Then the steps
came faster, and I realized that they were
trying to catch me. Almost at a bound
the first one caught my cloak. I stepped
away from it and darted on. I was too
frightened, too weak to cry out — I ran
on blindly. I felt that my skirt was
caught. I think I screamed then. But
at that moment two forms loomed up in
front of me. They were Uncle Williams
and Aunt Susanna. With a new effort I
threw myself into Susanna's arms. The
heavy old man lunged forward, struck my

pursuer down, then began to pound him with his fists.

" Lord Almighty, you sneak, Julian, what are you up to now?" he cried. "Get out of this!" It was really Julian Carlos, but he struggled up and ran away — he is so lithe and quick.

I was trembling from fright, so these kind souls took me back to their home, and put me in an outdoor hammock, where I rested quietly till the priest and Madame Conard came.

Adela was full of talk as usual. She bent over me and whispered,

" The little one that went to God," she said, " has sent another soul back into this unhappy world." Then she laughed merrily.

" So the Lord gives and the Lord taketh away." I was shocked at such levity, and, being weak and nervous, I could not restrain myself: I burst into tears and told them of my adventure. The Padre and Adela talked a while excitedly in Spanish, of which I understood a little.

"It is a revenge on account of that boat ride," they seemed to be saying. Then they said they would go back to look for my cloak. But they did not find it. When they returned the priest comforted and quieted me. He said it was a trick of Julian's to frighten some one; that he probably did not recognize me at all. But the Padre said, I should never go out alone anyway.

Then we came home, and Adela was so kind as to stay with me all night.

I must close this letter — Margarite is waiting to take me to Adela Villa, where I am to spend the day, and meet a young señora who wants to learn to paint. I shall be so glad to teach her.

Write me all the home news. And embrace our dear mother lovingly for me.

PAULA.

Chapter XI

The Venezuela Bonds

(The Padre's Notes)

June 28. I believe that serious trouble is coming to my little friend, the Countess of Villemaceda. It worries me greatly. I can see the meshes they are trying to entangle about her feet; if I am permitted, incidentally, to help unweave them, I am thankful; but I cannot be with her always, and I cannot tell what plot they may be laying to try to ruin her hopes or to get her away from the country. Lavandier even went so far as to go to the Governor of Samaná with a vile story, that the woman was not legally married to Curzoñ, that he picked her up on the streets of New York. But the Governor is a good man, a Catholic, a friend of mine, and he came to me to learn the truth. I was glad I happened to have the written history of herself, that the countess had prepared for me.

She has gained so many friends, and receives so much attention from our few dignitaries here, that more active animosity will be surely incited against her.

I am very positive that an attempt was made to abduct her from the Island the night before last. For what purpose, I know not — probably to ship her to New York by some South American vessel en route.

I thought it no risk to take her with me out to the old sugar mill to aid Madame Conard and myself with charitable duties to the living and the dead; I thought it would be a help to her by changing for a time the subjects of her thoughts.

But while I was busy in the old loft, the thoughtless little woman ventured out alone, and was actually pursued by Julian Carlos, and only accidentally saved by the fact that Uncle Williams and Aunt Susanna were coming through the thicket to offer their help to Madame Carter.

When Madame Conard and I arrived at the Williams' palenca on our way home, we found our friend in a pitiable condition of fright. I had noticed that the *Alondra*, a merchant ship belonging to Lavandier, was anchored in the bay, and I went immediately back to the shore to assure myself of the thoughts that came to my mind. As I expected, the canopied boat from the House of Palms lay close to the side of the *Alondra;* some conversation was being carried on and I recognized the voice of Lavandier.

It is evident that Julian Carlos knew of our trip to the sugar mill, and the *Alondra* happening to be on hand, the plan of abduction was at once conceived and the action taken. Uncle Williams and Aunt Susanna are not of my faith, but they are good simple souls. Thanks be to God for their fortunate presence in the thicket!

But I thought best to comfort the countess, to free her mind from its be-

wilderment.   She will be more calm not
to know all, and Madame Conard and I
will hereafter keep closer watch of her.

*   *   *   *   *   *

Margarite troubles me again.   Another
summer is being added to her years.   She
is beautiful.   I see her stop sometimes
on the street to pass a word with Julian.
I do not like that.   I gave her liberty to
attend the Señora de Curzoñ, but she
takes far too much liberty for herself.
Possibly she already loves him.   Determined to sound the depths of her foolish-
ness, I called her this morning from her
errand to market to come into my house.

" Margarite," I said severely, "why did
you run and tell Julian that the señora
had gone with Madame Conard to the
sugar mill ? "   The suddenness of my
attack disarmed her.

" Oh, Padre, what harm was that ? "

" It might be great harm," I said.
" Don't you know that he is her enemy ? "

" Oh, no, Padre, he says she is a lady."

" Yes, yes," I said, " and a lady that
stands in the way of Mercedes and Felix.

Margarite, you must not be talking to Julian. He means no good thing to you. He is only getting information out of you. I know what that conceited fool is thinking of, he thinks he can marry Mercedes — that is the reward he is working for."

Her head dropped, and drooped lower: she turned away. I kept silent, watching her. I saw the tears tremble on her cheek and fall; then with an affrighted look at me she snatched her market basket and ran out.

I have given her due warning. I hope she will profit by the advice.

July 1. The position of Señora de Curzoñ is growing serious. I know the character of Lavandier. His actions have not been without purpose. He has failed in mild measures — he may now be trying something else.

Little Julia came to me this morning in much distress. Her mistress had been taken suddenly ill. I went down and relieved her, leaving her comfortable and happy, but I, myself, came away verily troubled.   She had been taken ill directly after early breakfast.   I found symptoms of poisoning, and I also learned from Julia, that Julian had been about the kitchen that morning.

I will see the American consul to-night. We will advise together as to what should be done.   The unfortunate American woman needs protection.   I understand these people too well.

July 2.   A tall man in a full round cloak followed me into my room from the street.   He quietly seated himself in one of my stiff chairs by my table and waited for me to speak.   I closed the door and shutters and lit some candles.   He loosened his cloak.

"You were looking for me, Caccavelli," he said.

"No," I said, "I have ceased to look for any good from you, Don Luis." He flinched slightly.

"But I presume," I continued, "that between Margarite and Julian, you have heard of my consultation last evening with the American consul?"

"Or," he said, shrugging his shoulders, "Madame Conard may have whispered it to the wind."

"So you have come to protest," I continued; "would you have her die there in that house, a virtual prisoner, surrounded by her enemies?"

"If she is a prisoner, so am I," he broke in.

"But," I said, "I fear for her life, she will be poisoned."   Don Luis laughed.

"Caccavelli, you are an old maid. They will attempt nothing of the kind. Knaves are always cowards.   Besides Lavandier considers himself a gentleman. He is thinking of outward appearances. Madame Conard tells a story that makes the captain of the *Alondra* a kidnapper. I do not believe . that.

"But you need not take my wife out to the woods after dark, good Padre.   It was your fault."   He commanded my silence with a gesture, and then offered me a cigar.

"However, Caccavelli, I do not come to protest.   Quite the contrary.   I think it a very good plan.   You go ahead, and

institute a suit for a separate maintenance, a suitable establishment, and two
servants, that will be all right. She will
be comfortably fixed by herself, I suppose
somewhere near her beloved Madame
Conard. She will be my wife still; she
will be safer as you say, and there she
can stay until this damnable plot wears
itself out, and some day I may be able to
outwit the devil who has charge of us,
and throw myself at her feet to pray for
mercy — just go ahead, Padre, you have
my blessing."

I looked at him in astonishment. His
coolness was much of it forced, I knew
that.

"And you will permit that little woman
to suffer all this?" I said. He was calmly
lighting and drawing a cigar.

"That dear little woman is standing it
very well," he said; "she and Madame
Conard are out in the canopied boat at
this minute having a moonlight ride."

I brought down my hands with great
force on the table, as I gave vent to my
feelings.

"Don Luis, you are a coward!" I cried.

He smoked on as if in thoughts, for some moments.

"Dr. Caccavelli," he said dispassionately. "Did you happen to know anything about those Venezuela bonds? No? I supposed not. Well, I had a spare $80,000 at one time. Lavandier arranged a loan for me to General Pulgar and the Venezuela Government. You think it will never be paid? Oh, yes it will. The General Benacis Pulgar and Lavandier are bosom friends. I will get my money, but only through the influence of Lavandier. One does not care to fight a man who holds the key to $80,000, when time will make things all right anyway, eh Padre? My interest due on the $80,000 would remodel your old mission here, very comfortably." He paused and looked up at the ceiling. "There is only one thing I fear. You may have trouble with your suit. Lavandier doesn't want her comfortably maintained on this island, or any other. He wants her back in the States,

where she will get discouraged, and get
a divorce according to the laws of her
country."

He arose, wrapping his cloak about
him.

"Holy Marie! How wretchedly I
feel to-night! We are going to have a
thunder-storm. It is so close I can
hardly breathe. Buenas noches, Padre."

He was suffering, and in pain, I could
see that. I would have offered him a
remedy, but before I could speak he was
gone. He used to have alarming attacks
with his heart: I hope the excitement of
this trouble will not cause them to return.

Chapter XII

The False Interpreter

(The Padre's Notes)

June 29. I repaired this morning to the house of the American consul.

We sent for Señora de Curzoñ, and held a long consultation, at which we decided that the Doña Pauline should place herself under the protection of the court, and institute a suit for a separate maintenance, based on the evident absence of domestic peace, and conjugal relations, and the presence, in her husband's household, of those who were manifestly her natural enemies and were seeking to do her personal harm.

I thought best to impart to the Doña Pauline the substance of the conversation of her husband with me the previous evening. A new brightness lit up the pallor of her face, and she surrendered herself without reserve to the plans of Consul Conard and the lawyer we had summoned.

I do not think she realizes the gravity of the situation, nor did she comprehend much of our consultation, which was carried on in Spanish.

She knows that an arrangement was to be made by which she would have a cottage near her beloved Madame Conard, and be away from the presence of the Señor Lavandier — and that was about all.

In fact, before we had finished discussing the details, Madame Conard summoned some rowers, and she and the Señora Pauline went out on the bay in the canopied boat.

As I do not wish to be too much involved in the case, we decided to base the suit only on the fact of the virtual separation, and the circumstance that the Señor Lavandier had almost forced the countess to leave Samaná, and had given her five hundred pesos for that purpose, the details of this affair being already well known about town.

E. Contreas, our lawyer, judges the case to be plainly covered by the law.

July 10. To-day the Señora de Curzoñ formally placed herself under the protection of the court.

The case is set for the 20th inst., and Lavandier has already secured Apolo de Castro, the shrewdest lawyer on the island of San Domingo, for his counsel.

Don Luis walks the streets silent, pale, and self-contained, as oblivious to the busy hum of gossip that pervades the town as if he were a king sojourning here but for a day.

And verily, he has ruled this little end of the island, through his mercantile affairs, for so long, that he has no consideration for any one's opinion. He seems to be looking far over our heads; but his heart, his real heart is in Paris, and he lives only for the time when he can take his fortune there, and grace his life with his sweet and accomplished wife, whom I believe he loves and admires.

July 20. The case of the Señora de Curzoñ was quietly presented to-day before the Judge of the Tribunal of the 1st inst. of Samaná. We had kept the matter as private as possible, and there were few spectators.

I visited Don Luis in his library in the morning and found him to be too ill to appear—he was seriously prostrated and did not leave his room for several days after.

The Señora de Curzoñ appeared carrying herself with unusual grace and dignity. There was a bright color on her cheeks, and she wore some sort of a lace gown that gave her a most elegant appearance.

Truly, I reflected, so much does a little hope of love revivify a woman. Madame Conard, who was with her, showed much concern and nervousness; but the Doña Pauline flashed her soft eyes at me and smiled.

Julian Carlos, dressed like a fop, and wearing an unusual amount of jewellery, occupied the seat of honor with Lavandier, and appeared to be making continual suggestions to de Castro, the lawyer.

When we were all seated, the señora's council stood up and stated her case simply.

Then I gave my testimony, showing that an effort had been made to force the countess from her home, and showed also as plainly as I dared, that an attempt to poison her had been made. The testimony of Madame Grand, the housekeeper at the House of Palms, then showed that a virtual separation existed between Don Luis and his wife. Madame Conard and Margarite also gave testimony to the same effect.

Lavandier listened to the proceedings impassively.

When our testimony was in, the countess made the few simple statements we had planned for her to make; then the judge, to our great surprise, adjourned the court till the next day.

The American consul was very angry.

" It is quite evident," he said, as we went out, " that they had already arranged to have the night, in which to conjure up some villanous defence."

July 21. And verily they have succeeded well — so well, that only through some miracle of God to place motives of justice in the heart of a Samaná judge can my little friend hope to escape from the miserable consequences of this unhappy suit. The people here, who know of no laws but ours, will receive impressions that can never be wholly erased.

The counsel for the defence, the Señor de Castro, first stated that the Señorita Wright was not and could not be declared a lawful wife, for the reason that her marriage was neither civil nor ecclesiastical, it having been neither attested before a magistrate or solemnized by a priest of the true church.

Que Lastima! (What a pity!) As much as I regret that the señora is not a devotee of the true church, and sorrow that she could not have been married as a dear daughter of the faith, yet by the laws of the United States she is a wife, and there is a God of Justice who recognizes the true intent of these cases.

Eso es terrible! No one can tell how the judge will regard this matter.

Then a merciless attack was made on the lady's character. Captain Gavard of Lavandier's ship the *Alondra* testified with all the coolness of a paid liar, that when he was out walking in the woods on the evening of June the 22d, that he had been boldly accosted by the accomplished adventuress, Pauline Wright, and that upon her hearing the approach of her companions she had fled in haste, forgetting her cloak, which he had been carrying politely for her, and which article he now begged to return. Whereupon he unfolded the lost circular garment pertaining to the night's adventure, and with mock courtesy handed it over to the countess. And she, not understanding a word of this testimony in Spanish, received it with a smile of thanks.

The spectators, who were more numerous to-day, looked at each other with confirming nods.

The countess was here called to the chair of the witness, and Julian Carlos stood up in serene self-assurance to act in the office of interpreter to the court.

While the Señor de Castro was making his preliminary movements, a young man, a stranger to me, came in and took a seat beside me, where I sat in a back corner of the room.

He was quite fine looking, with a vigorous cast in general, and he removed a soft, jaunty steamer-hat. He fixed his attention immediately on the countess, and in fact we were all breathless, waiting for the proceedings of the Señor de Castro.

Then ensued a very extraordinary event for these sleepy island courts, and preceded by the most villanous and dastardly example of interpretation I have ever seen attempted.

I will record the conversation as it occurred:

Sr. de Castro (in Spanish). "Señorita, did you have a pleasant trip with the Count of Villemaceda from New York to Curaçoa?"

The Señora. "I enjoyed the trip with my husband exceedingly."

The Translation. "I enjoyed the company of the count."

Sr. de Castro. " Did you not become very well acquainted with Captain Benton of the *Yarrow ?* "

The Señora. " I did, he was very kind."

The Translation. " Captain Benton paid me attentions."

Sr. de Castro. " What do you think of Captain Benton ? "

The Señora. " I think of him as a very dear friend."

The Translation. " He was my lover."

Sr. de Castro. " Then you did not go ashore at Curaçoa at all ? "

The Señora. " Certainly, Señor, the Judge, I went ashore to my husband's house."

The Translation. " Certainly not, Judge, the captain had no house."

Here, Madame Conard and I were standing on our feet amazed and horrified, and the spectators were stirring with excitement, when with a bound the strange young man at my side left me and sprang into the middle of the room. He saluted the judge with a wave of his hat, and

began speaking to him in very clear
Spanish.

"Your honor, the Judge of this court,
that black devil who is interpreting is
telling you a pack of lies. He is not
giving her answers at all. And I want
to tell you and all the good people here
that the Countess of Villemaceda did go
ashore to her husband's house at Curaçoa,
for I was there by the house on the
lagoon in my merchantier, the *Petrel*,
that is now anchored out in this bay.
Not only myself, but my captain, and
all my men, saw the lady go to the
stone mansion, where she was appropriately received. Furthermore, I heard the
Señor Lavandier swear on the wall that
day that he would soon do away with
that American wife. I know that I am
out of place, but I can't sit here and see
such injustice perpetrated. Kick that
man out of this court, your honor, and I
will interpret for you."

But the little room had now lost all
its resemblance to a court of justice.
Lavandier had advanced upon the young

stranger, and Henry Conard stood between them.

Julian had sprung from the window, Madame Conard was up on her seat, clapping her hands, and confusion pervaded the room.

Our lawyer, in unwise haste, thinking that this was as good rebuttal as we could have, submitted the case, and the judge dismissed the court.

Henry Conard rescued the countess, his wife, and their maids from the crowd, and they, together with the stranger, went up to the consular residence.

There the countess will learn the cause of the exciting termination of her suit, and will be able in person to thank the gallant young master of the *Petrel*.

Chapter XIII

Bay Views

(A Letter)

THE ADELA VILLA,
Aug. 10, 18–.

MY DEAR NELL: — By this time you will know through my letter, and the letter the dear Padre was so kind as to write to you, all about my situation here and my singular suit with my husband, or rather, with that fierce old don, the Señor Lavandier, whom the Padre calls "the old Wolf."

We are waiting for the judge to give the decision in my case. My life goes on about the same, but with somewhat more of brightness and pleasure. I do not stay so much at the gloomy old House of Palms. It is my legal residence, however, and I have to stay there at night, accompanied by my two maids and sometimes Madame Conard. I frequently ap-

144

pear at dinner, where everything passes
off with the usual silence and decorum.

The days I spend at the consular residence. Early each forenoon I go to the
Padre's house to take a Spanish lesson.

After the Padre has helped me, he
enjoys having me read English to him.
While I do that, he generally has his
breakfast, which consists always of a cup
of black coffee and a slice of bread, cut
in small squares and brought to him in a
napkin. I wish I could send you a picture
of him as I see him sitting by his plain
table, his long black cassock tied with a
heavy cord, his pointed cap on, and his
kind and generous-looking face intent on
what I am reading. Every one here
loves the good old man ; all strangers of
affairs call on him, and every sea captain
comes ashore with a desire to see the
famous curate. He is so fatherly and
good to me !

*　　*　　*　　*　　*　　*

Some days we have very lively times at
the Adela Villa. Madame Conard nearly
always has company when there is a

L

steamer in the harbor, and, as many people from far and near have heard of me and my troubles, I am the object of much curiosity.

One day there were two brides here from Porto Plata; I helped Madame Conard to entertain them. I wore my long white lace dress, and Fred Olcott said I looked quite like a bride myself.

I must tell you all about Fred Olcott, for you must wish to know something of the young man, who so boldly helped me out at the trial.

Mr. Olcott is an American, a merchant from New York, and he is establishing trading-ports for his firm at four different places in this island. He is stationed here now doing some business for the interior. He controls the movements of a little merchant ship, the *Petrel*, with which he sometimes sails. He happened to be at Curaçoa when I was there, so that he immediately interested himself, when he had heard of my suit here.

He was the one who threw me the American apple, stuffed with a little note of warning, that I thought so absurd. He is such a breezy, pleasant young man, and he is as cheering to my daily life, as the kind Padre's good counsels are to my hopes.

He insists in helping Mr. Conard with my case, copying and recopying papers, and translating letters and documents. He goes to see the old judge nearly every day, to remind him that I am awaiting the decision and my papers. He says he thinks the judge is in collusion with my enemies; but I do not know exactly what that means.

Notwithstanding all this anxiety and trouble, my life goes on as I have said, very well. We often spend the evenings on the balcony at the consulate. Madame Conard receives callers informally then, and Fred Olcott comes often.

One day last week he boarded a steamer and bought a few early American apples.

In the evening he appeared on the balcony and dropped one over my shoulder into my lap. Then he instantly snatched it and threw it away.

"I beg your pardon, Señora," he said, "I am very thoughtless." I knew what he meant. It had brought back to me instantly that happy day in Curaçoa.

But I controlled my tears and smiled upon him.

"Never mind," I said, "I will believe your stuffed apple another time."

"Then I'll put a revolution in the next one," he said.

"What's that?" I asked.

"That, that," he said, "that's a process by which they remove their enemies and upset every one's plans. Then we Americans go home where we belong." He caught his breath and snatched his hat.

"There I am again! Please forgive me, Señora Pauline. I guess I am a little off this evening."

We tried to call him back, but he would not return.

That's Fred.

    *   *   *   *   *   *

Sometimes when the sunset is fair, I send a rower for my canopied boat, and

Adela and I go out on the bay and are rowed about during the long exquisite summer twilight.

Yesterday afternoon Fred accompanied us to Clara Bay, a dainty little inlet a few miles off.

We were easily landed on the clean, shell-covered beach, and while Madame Conard and Margarite prepared the lunch, Mr. Olcott found for me a cool seat beneath the fringing foliage of the shore. He then threw himself at my feet, and resting his elbow in his hat, he told me of his mother and sister in New York. I listened dreamily, conscious all the time of the gentle washes of the tide, and the calling of the gay birds in the cocoa-nuts over our heads.

I could not help enjoying myself and forgetting my perplexities. I naturally feel at home with Fred Olcott, he is so much more like my own people than any other person here.

When we were returning at sunset, Madame Conard and I lay back among the cushions, and even Adela was impressed to silence by the dreamy loveliness of the scene in the island-studded bay. Natives were passing noiselessly in their light canoes; a red mist came over the transparent green waves; the hilltops seemed to hang over the dense purple shadows, while the forest line lay between like a solid green fire.

Mr. Olcott suspended his witticisms to quote from the poets. A long blaze of golden light lay on the water under the western sun. I had a quiet feeling that at the end of that path, somewhere, lay love and happiness for me.

*   *   *   *   *   *

While I think of it, I must tell you that there is to be a grand ball in a fortnight, to celebrate a visit of the President of San Domingo to this state or district. I have an invitation, and have decided to go with the American consul and his wife. Mr. Olcott wishes to go with us. It will be a chance for me to see something of society here. I will copy my invitation for you. Mr. Olcott says he will wager his hat that I cannot translate it; but that is not necessary — you will prefer the Spanish.

La Señora de Curzoñ, La Condesa de Villemaceda:

Los que suscriben á nombra del Ilustre Ayuntamiento de esta localidad, tienen el honor de invitar á Vd. para un baile que tendra lugar en el Salon de la Aduana el dia que llegue á esta Ciudad S. E. el Presidente de la República.

Esperamos que, con su asistencia, su amabilidàd dará mas realce al deseo que nos anima.

Somos de Vd. afectisimos Segures Servidores   Q. B. S. M.

J. A. Lavana, H. Duguela, G. Lalaume.

Samaná el 24 de Agosto, 18–.

Adios, for to-day, dear sister.

*　　*　　*　　*　　*　　*

Aug. 20, 18–.

DEAREST NELL:— I will sit down to thank you for the budget of home news that I received to-day on my return from a delightful trip, which I will tell you of before other things occur to be noted down for you.

The Catholics had a great day at Savana del Mar, thirteen miles from here on the bay shore. The Padre went over several days previous, and Madame Conard and I the day before. We went in a large row-boat with several Spanish ladies and their servants. The Padre has a mission-house at Savana del Mar, which we occupied. I attended mass and tried earnestly to understand the ceremonies.

In the morning the Padre joined our party, and we returned home.

We started before the break of day, to avoid being out in the torrid noon, and so it was that I had the rare pleasure of seeing the sun rise on Samaná Bay.

The sky was a soft, tender blue, as exquisite as you might think the sky of Paradise to have been, and it seemed low and protecting, like a pale, daintily-frescoed ceiling. The sea was a kind of dove color, but clear and glittering. Our four rowers pulled us over rapidly and smoothly. A greenish yellow haze lay on the horizon. As the sunlight began to appear, blue and gold lights quivered over the currents of the tide, and shoals of flying fish, like bits of pearls, glittered through the undulations of the waves. We were in sight of the shore all the time, and the spice-laden air of the forest was wafted out to us. When the sun came up, the gray lines of trees turned to deep green, the hills took on bright colors, while the savannas between were veiled in vapors. Then the little becalmed ships lifted their white wings to catch the breeze, which blew away also a bank of mist, and I saw the red-tiled roofs of Samaná. I have since found a quotation, which describes the scene perfectly:

" Long on the waves the morning mists reposed,
Then broke, and, melting into light, disclosed
Half-circling hills, whose everlasting woods
Swept, with their sable skirts, the shadowy floods."

You can easily imagine, my dear sister, how refreshed I was when I stepped on shore from this almost idyllic voyage.

I felt revivified and hopeful, ready to be patient and cheerful while the days of waiting go on. The *Thybe* has come into the bay and I must close this letter.

Your far away sister,

PAULA.

Chapter XIV

The President's Ball

(A Letter)

THE ADELA VILLA,
Aug. 25, 18–.

THE ball is over. I am not yet rested from a strange experience I have had and the excitement of it all. It will quiet my nerves to write you about it. Madame Conard and Margarite helped me to dress. I wore my white brocade silk that I have worn but once before: that was on my reception day in New York.

They rolled my hair high in puffs, and managed in some way to suspend from it a black Spanish veil. Then they floated more black lace from my skirt and down over the long train, and I was quite surprised myself at the effect. I took my large white fan in my hand, and walked into the parlor to meet Fred Olcott. Without a moment's hesitation, he knelt at my feet, at a graceful distance, and kissed the tip feathers of my fan.

" You should be an English duchess ! " he said.

Adela had a sudden fit of laughter over this, and ran off to get ready. Do you think it was any harm for me to let Fred button my gloves for me ? I don't. He is so gentlemanly, and as frank and as natural as a brother.

The ball was held in a large, low, unfinished building; but it was finely decorated with flags of all nations, palms, and the wonderful greeneries of this exotic land. All Samaná was there, that is, all of the higher classes, — the professional and official people, the merchants, and the dons and doñas from the plantations of the locality.

The President and suite sat on a platform, and were quite American looking, save for the profusely dressed, dark-eyed señoras who were in the background.

Our party must have made a sensation, when we went in, for the people parted right and left to look at us. We walked around the room, and then took seats against the wall.

Lavandier was there, more dignified than ever, and walking with him was that handsome man I met in the forest, Don Juan Portola.

I could not remove my eyes from him, and very soon Adela pressed my arm, and told me that I must not stare. My curiosity was gratified, however, for Don Juan left Lavandier and had an interview with Mr. Conard, who presented him to me.

Don Juan speaks English well, and his voice is soft and rich.

I was charmed with him, and all Fred Olcott could do was to walk away. Don Juan took the vacated seat.

"I am truly delighted," he said, "leaning deferentially towards me, "that you have concluded to grace Samaná society. You are the only lady, by virtue of title, here, and you really owe us this condescension. You are a diamond among pebbles, Señora."

"Oh, no," I cried, annoyed at his presumption. "I am here only to observe. I cannot enter society: my situation prevents it. I do not want the admiration of these people. I wish only their respect. Besides, I do not understand your manners and customs."

He smiled.

"You would soon learn everything," he said. "Now if you will come with me, I will show you through this stately Spanish dance — a quadrille, you would call it in America."

I looked at him in surprise.

"No, I thank you, Señor," I said in a more reserved manner; "I do not intend to dance. You should know that I would not."

His handsome face clouded a little, and soon after he made the most polite adieus to Madame Conard and myself and went away.

I noticed that he joined Lavandier, and they disappeared together. I drew a long breath to release my fascinated senses, when who should step up beside me, but Don Luis, my husband. Instantly, I recognized the fact that the two men possessed the same powers of instantaneous fascina-

tion. I could not think at all, I was so surprised ; but Don Luis was amazingly cool.
He threw his arm back of me gracefully,
and leaning over near me, said slowly :

"Pauline, you are my wife ; you have
perfect liberty to do as you please, as I
told you. But I want to protect you from
all real dangers. That Olcott is all right—
he is as harmless as a pretty dog. Don't
think I am such a fool as to be jealous of
him ; besides, you have a right to flirt, if
you choose, under the exasperating circumstances. But I beg of you, Pauline, do
not receive the attentions of such men as
Portola. Lavandier sent him : do not
trust him. My Condesa, come, let us
dance."

I had no power to refuse. In an instant, to the amazement of all near us, we
were gliding around in the soft motions
of a waltz, and he was pouring into my
ears the old passionate words of the happy
days. There were no other dancers : they
do not waltz here, but they were then
marching to a slow waltz interlude. Oh,
what happiness for a few moments ! Then

his arm loosened, he swayed away from my side, and several men caught his drooping form. Don Luis had fainted!

Lavandier and Julian pressed in and carried him out of the crowd. No one spoke to me, but I caught my train up in my arm, and struggled out of the confusion to the door.

When I got out, I did not know where I was; I lost my way; but I kept running until I found the entrance to the House of Palms.

When I reached the house they were just going in — he had recovered and was walking. I wanted to be with him so much; I was newly brave, I followed. I reached the door of his room behind them. Then, when Lavandier saw me, he pushed me back with his long arm, and closed the door in my face.

I sank down trembling, hoping in my poor heart that I would still be let in, but Madame Conard found me, and told me it was very immodest, and very unwise for me to remain there. So I came back to the cottage. They have kept me in my bed all day. I have been thinking and thinking.

Don Luis was surely overcome by some strong emotion. He loves me, I know that. But he is jealous of Don Juan Portola — he surely is. It is pure jealousy, nothing else. I hope I will meet Portola again. He might bring Don Luis to me once more.

I am glad something moves his iron nerves. With fondest love, and do not worry so much about me, my dear sister.

Affectionately,

PAULA.

M

Chapter XV

At Old San Domingo

(A Letter)

THE ADELA VILLA,
Sept. 1, 18–.

MY DEAR SISTER : — I have been in a miserable condition of apathetic despair all day, and my poor friend Adela has been hovering over me, one moment in tears, the next in a passion of anger.

Fred Olcott has been running back and forth carrying news, and the consul and my lawyer have been shut up for several hours in the library.

Yesterday the report came to the cottage that Don Luis was ill. I was determined to go down, but Adela held me, and Fred Olcott stood with his arms across the open doorway.

While I was hesitating, the consul called me to the upper balcony. We saw the ship *Alondra* standing close to the

shore, and the canopied boat was going
out to it.   I ran for the marine glasses.
Don Luis was leaning among my cushions, and Lavandier and Julian were with
him.

Lavandier returned alone, and the
Alondra put out to sea.   Then Fred
Olcott went down to the street, and found
that Don Luis had been sent to Curaçoa
on a business trip and for the benefit of
his health.   I said I was glad for that part
of it, but Fred laughed and said:

" There's something in the wind, you
will see.   I'll have to get you another
American apple stuffed! "

So this morning I was called down to
court, and the judge read his decision,
which was translated to me.   When it
was over I rose with all the dignity I
could command, took Mr. Conard's arm,
and walked home.

For a while I sat dumb with grief, in
my chair, then dear Adela coaxed me into
a great basket-chair on the balcony, and
she and Olcott wearied themselves trying
to divert me.

Good old Uncle Williams and Aunt Susanna came with a basket of lovely and delicious summer fruits, and I could not help rousing up and thanking them.

But, O my dear sister, my suit has failed utterly. They have accepted the defence; it is a non-suit, and as I am not a legal wife, I can have no rights except such as they may allow me as a sort of dependant at the House of Palms.

The judge referred me to my own country, where my so-called marriage took place, and suggested that there I might be able to obtain redress for my grievances.

How skilfully it was all planned! Don Luis was sent away that he might not come to my rescue, if he wished.

The Padre has been up to see me.

" My poor little unfortunate," he said, placing his hand on my head. " Unfortunate, but not so unfortunate as those who sin against you, for the God of Heaven will surely punish them."

*   *   *   *   *   *

Evening. My lawyer and the consul have decided to appeal to the Supreme Court of San Domingo, and the Padre heartily approves of the plan. We all approve, and I am trying to be happy and cheerful.

The consul says that the Supreme Court will be more likely to have some respect for the laws of the United States, and that Lavandier will not have so much power there.

It seems that there is a sort of French law on the statutes by which I might be able to obtain a divorce, if necessary, and Fred says that *that* is the thing to do. But the Padre shook his head, and so did I.

*   *   *   *   *   *

September 2. It is decided that I must go to the city of San Domingo myself to take my papers and explain my case to a lawyer there. Margarite will go with me. My money that the Padre has been keeping for me is of great use now.

I may be away two weeks. I will take my letter with me to write you when I get to the city.

*   *   *   *   *   *

San Domingo, September 6. I came here on the English steamer, which dropped anchor in our harbor last Sunday afternoon. The Conards took me out to the steamer in their boat, and the Padre went with us. When we were alongside the steamer the good old curate placed his hand on my head, and said, "God will take care of you. Have courage, I will pray for you."

The consul introduced me to the captain and the doctor on the steamer, and then I was waving my handkerchief and watching my kind friends as they rowed away. But I saw them through my sudden tears, as one sees through a trembling veil.

I was then so oppressed by the misery of my situation, that I went to my room where I should not need to restrain my tears.

All the English Margarite could think of to say was, "Pobre Señora. So many love you! Do not cry, little one."

I diverted myself by making my very best travelling toilet for the five o'clock dinner. I was glad of my pains when I was given the seat of honor between the captain and the doctor. Then my heart jumped to my throat, when I saw enter, and sit down opposite me, that handsome don I had met at the ball, the Señor Portola. I know the blood flamed to my cheeks, for I had not forgotten his association with my last adventure, and I was again conscious of his powers of fascination, and the charm of his perfect figure and polished manners. Our eyes met, and he bowed gracefully.

He greeted the captain and doctor familiarly, as if he might be very well acquainted with them. Then he turned to me, —

"I heard that you were to be on the steamer," he said; "but you came on before I did."

"Are you going to San Domingo city, also?" I asked.

"Yes," he returned. "I have been called suddenly on business. I have a case in court there, involving over one hundred thousand dollars. From there I go to my home in Cuba. Chance is certainly kind to me to give me the pleasure of meeting you again."

I replied that I was pleased to know that some one I had met before was on the steamer.

Then the captain spoke to him, and the conversation became general.

The next morning the steamer went into the harbor of Porto Plata, and remained there nearly all day.

When I came on deck the captain met me, and talked with me some time, showing me all the points of interest around Porto Plata, and describing the quaint old town at the foot of the mountain slope.

The captain had occasion to leave me for a moment, and Don Juan Portola stepped to my side.

"Do you like this island scenery?" he said.

"How lovely it is!" I cried. "I would like nothing better than a home on this charming island."

"You should have your desire," he answered warmly.

I thought this rather personal, and felt slightly embarrassed. I turned about, and we began to pace the deck.

The breeze came in my face, my veil curled about my throat, and I felt a girlish sense of enjoyment in the romantic situation.

I hope the spirit of coquetry has not taken hold of my heart, like a foul weed in a fair garden, but I could not help wishing that Don Luis could have seen us.

"I know of the object of your journey," Don Juan said, a little later. "If I can be of any assistance to you, do not hesitate to let me help you."

He seemed to know all about my case, and expressed an interest in a most reserved and gentlemanly manner.

He said that being already in court, and well acquainted with the laws and customs here, he would be able to aid my cause very much. I tried to express my thanks appropriately.

"Every one is so kind," I said.

"How could they help being so!" he replied earnestly.

It was cool and clear, and very early in the morning when we came in sight of the famous old city of Columbus. It is near the sea, but it is built on the bank of the Ozama River. We had to leave the steamer and go up the river in boats. I was enraptured with the scene. Before me rose the ancient walls and turrets of the old Spanish era. They are time-scarred, and yellow, and festooned with mosses and vines. I felt as if I were about to be landed somewhere in the middle ages.

But on shore it was a modern West Indian scene. Diminutive donkeys, dirty urchins, half-naked negroes, lazy porters, and dusky girls, carrying baskets of fruits, filled up the narrow streets.

Don Juan and the captain accompanied me to the Hôtel de la Union, and placed me in the care of Madame Cloud, the landlady, who, with Margarite's aid, has made me very comfortable.

I had many letters of recommendation which, through the kindness of the captain, I was able to have sent out immediately.

There was one from the governor of Samaná to the president; the kind curate of Samaná had sent one to an influential friend; Mr. Conard had written to the consul here, and even Fred Olcott knew a merchant with whom to correspond in my behalf.

After the eleven o'clock breakfast, the lawyer, to whom our consul had written, called, and I gave him my documents and told him, through an interpreter, all that was necessary.

In the evening I had a sort of a reception on account of my letters of introduction. There was a jovial old English sea captain, Captain Guthrie, a friend of Mr. Conard's, who seemed like a father.

The consul and his wife brought the vice-consul, who is a Baltimore gentleman, and also the vice-consul from Azusa. There was Mr. Hatch, a correspondent of the New York *Tribune*, the Padre's friend (a planter), and several others.

"It is a grand event here," said Captain Guthrie to me, "to have so many English-speaking people get together.

These people are delighted to meet each other, and your advent here will long be remembered. I hope it will be the beginning of some sort of unity among the foreign residents."

*   *   *   *   *   *

That was last evening.

The Señor Portola called to-day to tell me how things are progressing in court. He advised me not to go to court myself, as it would be contrary to Spanish customs. He thinks my lawyer can do better without my presence. I wonder if I ought to trust him! Don Luis said I must not; but Don Luis was only jealous.

*   *   *   *   *   *

September 7. To-day I went with Captain Guthrie to see the old cathedral, the first Mausoleum of Columbus in the New World. It is constructed of stone, with the masonry eight feet thick in the walls. Its interior, with its many altars, pillars, and arches, is very impressive. The cross that Columbus brought with him is still here. I gathered some ferns and mosses from the ancient wall. We went also to see the remains of the Castle of Columbus, a house that was built by the son of the Admiral. The vines run riot over the old pile, but the ruins are noble, even in their decay.

* * * * * *

September 8. Mr. Hatch took me to-day to call on the president. Mr. Hatch is a fine, kindly old gentleman, full of good advice. He says he takes an interest in me for the sake of his dear daughters in New York. He has been some years in San Domingo, and on this account I thought him the best one to take me to the president.

The president took my hand and said, " I will do all in my power for you."

When we came away, Mr. Hatch said gravely, " Do not be too hopeful. I do not think our American women married abroad can do anything but submit in silence to their grievances."

" But," I said, " Mr. Hatch, I would have had to have gone home in disgrace, —an abandoned wife. I was in danger from my enemies."

He looked at me smilingly and said,
"I don't think anything could disgrace
you, my child."

*　*　*　*　*　*

September 9. I rose early this morning
and went with Captain Guthrie to walk
about this quaint old city. We ascended
to the top of the city wall, where we had a
very fine view of the river, the sea, the ancient fortifications, and the curiously built
town. Then we went to the Wall of Columbus, said to have been built by him. Our
walk was along the river side, which was
beautiful with all kinds of tropical foliage.

A shower came up, and we stepped into
a place where they were making rope, and
there the captain entertained me till the
shower was over with a long story about
a mutiny on the coast of Africa. To-
morrow the English steamer stops here,
and I can go back to Samaná.

My lawyer came in this afternoon and
says that I have done all that can be
done, and that it will be a month, at
least, before I can get a decision.

*　*　*　*　*　*

THE ADELA VILLA, Sept. 14.

With my last line I had spent my last peaceful, hopeful hour in San Domingo. The remainder of my stay was different. I have found that I should have heeded Don Luis' advice when he warned me against the Señor Portola.

That last evening after I had written you about the walk and the shower, Madame Cloud summoned me to the parlor. Don Juan Portola had called. He was elegant in every movement, and still as entertaining; but he seemed nervous. I tried to be bright and agreeable, but he was unresponsive.

He bent his handsome face in his hands, and I was almost as interested and troubled as if it had been Don Luis himself.

He rose abruptly saying, —

"Is there nothing more I can do for you before you go?"

I remembered that I wanted to go to the Franciscan Monastery, and as Captain Guthrie and Mr. Hatch had gone out of the city I spoke of it.

His face lighted up.

"You honor me!" he said.

So we arranged to go in the cool of the morning. Then it seemed to me all the night as if it might be morning. I could not sleep.

Margarite brought me my coffee, as usual, early in the morning; but when I was ready to go out I could not find her. So I joined Don Juan and went out alone with him.

My cheeks glow now with shame that I dared to do such a thing! He was not an American; it led him to misjudge me.

Besides, I know now that there are pitfalls for my innocent feet, and that Lavandier digs them.

I will tell you — but first I must tell you of our walk and the famous old monastery.

When I went under the great archway that leads into the grand old ruins, I clasped my hands and stood silent, so impressed was I with the unearthly grandeur and beauty of the place.

Only the great massive walls remained

of the once holy sanctuaries of the black-robed devotees.

Nature had usurped their altars. Waving banners of ferns and vines were planted on the highest walls, and the space was lighted by the broad light of the pure skies.

The interior was full of fruit trees of all kinds, and thousands of bees were at work. They had their hives in the many hollow logs that were lying in the enclosure.

This monastery was formerly very extensive. The Hôtel de la Union, where I stopped, was once one of the buildings. The nuns' cells still exist. They extend through two long streets, and have been at one time connected with the great church by six subterranean passages.

The Señor Portola told me of the strange legends connected with them as we forced our way through the vines and ferns to look into one of the passages which is still open. I shuddered to think of the weird stories these dark paths might tell if they could speak; then we turned back to the entrance.

N

I liked best to look at the fan plumes waving triumphantly heavenward.

I felt uneasy. I saw that Don Juan was regarding me intently and silently. So I led the way through the arched entrance and walked back to the hotel. I bade him good morning and hurried up the stairway to my room.

I had scarcely closed the door when it opened again, and Don Juan walked in and closed the door behind him. He had now a look of purpose and determination on his face. Then he snatched my hands and held them firmly. I could not move.

"What do you mean?" I cried. "Let me go."

"I mean that I love you, sweet Condesa," he said calmly. My tears started.

"O Señor," I pleaded, "have I not always showed myself a lady in every way? Is there the slightest reason that you should intrude on me so?"

"No, no," he said, "you have been a brave, modest, little esposa (wife). But I want to talk to you — to reason with

you. You please me, and the more I
see of you the more interesting you are
to me. You are so different from my
own country-women. Listen to me, do
not struggle, I shall not hurt you. I
have a beautiful home in Cuba. Leave
that unloving husband of yours and go
with me. I can make you happy; Don
Luis does not. You shall have everything that money can bring. You are
now forsaken and alone — far from your
own country and friends. Your husband
has practically abandoned you. After
this suit you can have no social position
in Samaná. In the United States your
name is ruined.

"I love you — come to me." He
paused, then I cried out, —

"Señor, release my hands." He let
them go, and took hold of my arm.
But he saw that I was not influenced
by his arguments.

"Listen, now," he went on. "You are
in my power. I have influence in this
court. If you will go with me, your case
will be decided in your favor. Before the

world you will be a vindicated wife. If you refuse, I will tell them that Julian's translation and Captain Gavard's testimony were the truth, — your case is lost, you are lost.

"Come, come, little sweetheart, come to me. And I ask you to come for love. Lavandier asked me to entice you away. But I now have another motive — it is my own love for you. If you refuse my heart and home, only a revolution could win your case."

"God will send a revolution then!" I cried. "No, no, my case may be lost, but I would not do wrong. I would not sin to save even my life. Leave me, Señor Portola, leave me now." Then he became angry.

"Who are you?" he cried passionately. "And where did you learn such virtue?"

My Bible, my Beloved Comforter, lay on the table. I seized it amid my tears, and cried, "Señor Portola, this Holy Book taught me, and the teachings of my noble father and mother." I held it over my head and looked at him with a high courage in my heart.

He then released my arm, made me a low bow, gave me a long passionate look, and left me without another word.

I fell on my knees and thanked my God. As the Padre had said, He had taken care of me. Then I prayed that justice might be done, and that the labors of my Samaná friends might not be frustrated by this deeply laid plan of Lavandier's, and the revenge of this passionate Spaniard.

That evening I bade good-by to the hotel guests, who had all treated me with the greatest courtesy and respect, and was rowed down the Ozama River to the anchored steamer.

My trip homeward was uneventful, and my lonely heart was glad when I saw dear Madame Conard in her little boat, coming out on the smooth Samaná waters to meet me.

Your unhappy sister,
PAULINE.

Chapter XVI

A Commission for the *Petrel*

(The Padre's Notes)

September 20.   Having written a few
letters of explanation to the sister of the
Señora de Curzoñ, I have been the recipient
of a number of letters from the United
States, and as this is one of the ways in
which I can aid the unfortunate American
woman, I have taken much interest in re-
plying to them.

I have felt it to be for the best that I
should encourage the mother and sister to
believe that the difficulties of my little
friend were but of a temporary nature.

I, who have known Don Luis for so
long, have observed that he has seldom
failed to reward those, whom he has caused
to suffer, in order that he might obtain some
object.   I pray that it may be so in this case.

I have replied carefully to the business-like inquiries of Judge Baker, the lawyer at Northham.   For the sake alone of her good name in America, she ought to win the case.   But I truly believe that the case and its outcome has no bearing whatever upon that which the eccentric Don Luis intends eventually to do.

Judge Baker has wisely engaged a prominent law firm in New York to work in conjunction with the señora's counsel at San Domingo, in order to put in action whatever outside influences that might be made to bias the Supreme Court in her favor.   However, I well know what stubborn facts will stand against the wise and efficient efforts of so great a law firm as Messrs. Butler, Stillman, and Hubbard, of New York.

As long as the tenure of office of governors, presidents, and judges is so uncertain, these dominicans naturally look to personal profit as the first cause of action. Why decide for justice, when one is to be put out of office by a revolution the next week?

However, such high-class legal interfer-

ence from New York has its social effect,
and it has enabled me to explain to my
people here that the American señora is
a lady of the highest respectability and
family in her own country.

One of the effects of this was that the
governor, the mayor, and other dignitaries of Samaná called upon her at the
American Consulate on the day of her
return from San Domingo; and the entire
company seemed not displeased when they
saw their Padre coming up through the
orange trees, to ask Madame Conard for
a cup of coffee, for I had been on a tire-
some walk in the country.

The little countess was very apprecia-
tive and entertaining to us all, and the
governor was so much pleased with her,
that he took my arm, and came with me
to my house, where he wrote a letter to
Miss Wright, her sister, — from which I
begged to make an extract for my records
of the señora's career in Samaná:

I can more or less imagine the sorrow
you and your family have felt through the

sufferings of your sister at this place, where she is a stranger far from home. But I hope she will soon be rid of the great grievances surrounding her. You may be assured that I shall be happy to be of service to her, and I hope to have the chance to prove myself a friend to the gentle American lady and her family. I have the honor to subscribe myself,

Your most humble servant,

F. RODRIGUEZ,
Governor of Samaná.

October 1. The *Alondra* dropped anchor in the bay yesterday, and her boats came in with Don Luis, Mercedes and her child, Julian Carlos, and several native servants.

I heard on the street that the Señora Pauline came down from the Consulate, threw open the House of Palms, and received Don Luis and his daughter-in-law with as much grace and affability as if she had been in all respects the mistress of the mansion. This sort of conduct is what she should have assumed from the first — a course of dignity, assumption, and disdain.

These qualities count for far more in these countries than sweetness and humility.

She did not remain a moment after the five o'clock dinner, however, as I saw her returning with Margarite to the Adela Villa.

Last evening when I came from the church to my office next the street, I surmised, by a light shining underneath the door, that Don Luis was there. No one else has the assumption to help himself to my candles.

He was sitting by my table. He was very pale, and lacked his usual strong and self-restrained expression. But he extended his white hand across the table and held mine firmly.

" Ah, Caccavelli, you are looking well ! Are you glad to see me back ? " he said.

I looked down upon him in silence. He knows that I am displeased with his conduct. When he released my hand, I went over to my drug cabinet, and opened it, intending to ignore him and put my mind on some duties there.

"Come, come, Padre," he said, "never mind your cordials: they cure no one anyway. Come and talk to me. I know you are blaming me. I shouldn't have gone away. Please, good friend, let me explain. I supposed that I was leaving things in very good shape. Señor Castro, the villain, promised me she would win the case. I crossed his palm with my purse, but there are bigger purses than mine, eh, Padre? Do you not find it so?" Here I poured him a little of my best wine, and sat down to give him my attention.

"You are condemned by every one," I said, "for allowing your wife to suffer these things. Why did you not take her, and go away to the States, Spain, anywhere —?"

"There, there, Caccavelli, I am tired of that," he interrupted. "A man of my habits can't run away to live on air. Besides, I don't propose to live on air. This situation was forced on me, and I am trying, as best I can, to get out of it with at least my bonds; and — and — I thought the wife would keep all right. I intend to succeed, Padre. I have had no open quarrel with Lavandier: he thinks he is my master still.

"I favored this suit only to make things pleasant for her, for the time being, as you know. That it has turned out disastrously is another matter. I had to go to Curaçoa when I did — there was a buyer there for our property.

"You say I should have lost a buyer rather than have caused such suffering to my virtuous and innocent young wife?

"Well, I left my last peca for the judge. That is all I could have done had I been here."

Then he swallowed the wine I had poured for him, and lay back in his chair with a strange and hardened expression on his face. Then he hit the table a short, sharp rap with his pencil.

"Padre," he said, "here's a sou for all your trouble. The wife didn't keep. She's lost her patience and turned into

an adventuress.   Didn't you think it
strange that the Señor Portola went
with her to San Domingo?   Besides, —
hold, be patient, Padre, 'let me tell you.
I have had a fancy for collecting jewels.
My treasure was at the Curaçoa house.
I expected to get it, to help me out in
this matter.   Why, Captain Gavard would
swear himself a vile perjurer that he is
but for one bracelet to give Mercedes."
He paused.   "Well, Padre, the treasure
was gone.   The point is right here.   But
one person besides myself knew where
those jewels were, and that person was—"

He nodded towards the consul's hill.

"Your wife?" I cried.

"Yes, my 'virtuous and innocent young
wife,' — very!   Those jewels are worth
five thousand pesos.   What is she stay-
ing around here for when she has all
that to go with?"   Then I saw that he
was not in his natural mind.   Jealousy
and trouble had unsettled his power of
reasoning.   I resolved to undo the tangle.   His soul was sick, he needed a
violent remedy, and I resolved that he

should have it. I excused myself for a
moment, wrote a summons, and sent
my servant, Marie, with it to the Consulate.

When I returned his face had a softer
look.

"I was gradually getting things in
order," he said gloomily. "I sold the
Curaçoa property, and sent my portion
of it to my lawyer in Spain. This places
matters there on a sound basis. I had
arranged to buy myself from Lavandier
by confirming Felix the sole heir to all
that. I should soon have been free."
Then he laughed sarcastically. "But
it is all over now. I shall go to the
States and divorce her. One does not
care to have a sly, thieving adventuress
for a wife!

"That was a regular Yankee trick,
wasn't it, to get away with those jewels?
However, they were her's — the action
was but a certain, intuitive New England precaution. But this Portola affair, Padre, makes me sick! Lavandier
has the facts of the case from de Castro.

He saw them together. There is something about a visit to the Franciscan Monastery!"

Here he stopped, startled, for I was pointing my angry, trembling finger straight in his face.

"And who would blame her," I cried, "if she ran away with Portola — ?"

"Which you know, Dr. Caccavelli, I would never do!" cried the clear voice of the countess, and she entered the room enveloped in that famous round cloak, followed by the jaunty master of the *Petrel*, hat in hand.

Despite his unnatural state of mind, Don Luis rose with a bow of respect to his countess. He frowned upon the young American, who took no notice of him, but composedly seated himself in the corner as if he might have been there on business of his own.

The senora had heard her husband's last words. The kindly light that so often dominated her face faded into an expression of scorn and contempt. I concluded, from her look and manner,

that Don Luis had now committed a sin
which she would hold unpardonable.

"You sent for me, Padre?" She was
waiting for me to speak.

"Señora," I said, "in a certain manu-
script you gave me, a biography of yourself, you spoke of a tray of jewels. Now,
that matter was in confidence, and I should
never have spoken of it, but you are now
accused by your husband of having taken
those jewels. I would like the matter
cleared up. If you can be accused of
taking them so might I be. My knowledge of their existence stands against
me." I said this — more that Don Luis
might see the absurdity of his conclu-
sion.

In the silence that followed, I closely
watched the effect of my words upon him.
He suddenly shielded his face with his
hands and the color flamed up. He was
already ashamed of his unreasonable sus-
picion.

The señora did not speak; a look of
wild astonishment came over her face.
Then her features took on the cold ex-

pression of wounded pride, which faded into an aggrieved look; and then the droop of her eyes and the trembling of her lips showed that the outrageous wound to her honor would soon be expressed by a woman's best resource, — tears.   It was an oppressive situation, and I knew not how to relieve it.

Suddenly, Don Luis sprang up, took her hand gently, and put her down in his seat.

" Don't, don't, Pauline," he said kindly, " I was beside myself — with everything. Perhaps you think I do not suffer.   I have suffered more than I can bear, and retain my reason."

Here the young American stepped forward with considerable self-assurance.

" Perhaps I can throw light on this little difficulty," he said.

He produced a small package, and laid bare from its wrappings a fine, large pearl.   Don Luis examined it carefully.

" I would know it anywhere," he said. " It is one of mine."

" When I was down in Curaçoa last

June," continued the young man, "I
bought this for a silk handkerchief of a
crazy old creature on the wall. I have
been looking for its owner ever since."

Then the señora looked up at her husband with an expression of gladness.

"It must have been poor old Sheba,"
she said. "She was always hidden in a
corner of that room. She could have
been there that night." Señor Olcott
took a nervous, impatient turn across the
room and then spoke up.

"I am going down to Curaçoa soon,"
he said. "And for the sake of the
lady, I will undertake to get those
jewels, if they are not scattered all over
the island."

"And you may consider it a commission
from myself," said the countess. "I
know that you can get them if any one can
— you have so much ingenuity." Then
she turned to me with a radiant face.

"I thank you, Dr. Caccavelli, so very
much, for letting me know of this. I—"
she turned to Don Luis, as if she were
about to speak to him, but a cloud as of

pain and sorrow came down over her face,
and she turned away.

The master of the *Petrel* promptly put
on his hat and went out.

Don Luis took the hand of the countess and detained her a moment.

" Pauline," he said softly, " forgive me ;
do not add this to my crimes.   Give me
one kind word before you go."

Her face flushed, and for one moment
she looked as if she was about to step into
his arms.   Then she threw a startled look
at me and slipped away.

If Don Luis did look discomfited, he
certainly looked relieved.   And I concluded that the very sight of her pure face
had disburdened his mind of the Portola
matter also.   He said nothing, but sat by
the table, and rested his head heavily in
his hands.

Presently he rose, and walked out
slowly, as he might have been very tired.

The pearl was forgotten.   And as I
could get no one of the three to take it
afterwards, I eventually sold it to replen-
ish my stock of drugs for the poor.

Chapter XVII

The Embroidered Cushion

(A Letter)

The Adela Villa,
Oct. 4, 18—.

My Dear Sister :— There are more days of sorrow, even disgrace, for me. If my husband himself should come to my aid, he could not save me from this new distress and mortification. The news has come that I have lost my case at San Domingo city. How can I clear my good name now! The United States consul at Porta Plata came this morning from San Domingo, a passenger on the *Thybe*.

He has had some law business in San Domingo, and employed the same Señor de Castro, who is there for Lavandier. De Castro told him in a course of conversation that he was about to gain the case against me in all points.

The Conards have tried to soften the blow; they have been telling me that de Castro would be likely to say things like that, and that I must not despair until I have more definite news.

But my heart has gone out of me — the strain has been so long! I want to see home and mother; but I can not, I dare not come back home with the disgraceful defeat upon me! This is a strange country. There is one great power, however, and that is the church — if the good Padre were not my friend, and if my enemies were not afraid of him, I would have been crushed long ago.

But if I could only see my own New England home this morning. The tears start, when I think of the dear old sitting-room, and the armchair where father used to sit by the fireside, book in hand.

I have suffered much anguish in receiving letters of congratulations from friends at home, for I have told no one but you and Judge Baker of my trouble in this foreign land.

Don Luis, Mercedes, and Felix have

arrived from Curaçoa, and I suppose Lavandier is as happy as he is exultant.

Mercedes has been to call on me, here at the Consulate. She brought her beautiful boy, Felix: I wish I dared to love him.

Mercedes is very sweet, and talked to me very prettily through Madame Conard. She wonders why I do not stop at the House of Palms, and evidently does not know anything about my troubles.

Poor Margarite droops, and is not herself since Julian came. Madame Conard says that she is in love with Julian.

Poor simple child! She is a great care to the Padre, who says she will eventually throw away for love, and perhaps has already, all that his guardianship has acquired for her.

It is quite evident that Julian thinks that he can get Mercedes, and all the town is laughing at him. Captain Gavard is in love with her; but Mr. Conard says she is being reserved for some one of far greater importance, and that Lavandier will doff all these lovers when he is through with them.

I thank you, my dear sister, so much
for the velvet and embroidery silk you
sent. It has helped me to pass away
many uneasy hours; I am embroidering
a design for a cushion. I cannot tell
you how many sighs I tangle in with the
floss.

Fred Olcott seems to be very much
interested in the work, and frequently sits
by me to watch its progress. But he has
made a serious mistake and blunder, and
I am very much annoyed with him. Yesterday as I was sitting out in the balcony,
pencilling a figure on the velvet, he was
walking restlessly back and forth, and evidently counselling with Madame Conard,
who was out under the banana trees.

Finally he came and deliberately sat
down as close to me as he dared.

"Why don't you leave this miserable
country," he said; "what good will your
suit do you, even if you gain it? You
surely don't care for Don Luis now?"

"Please don't talk about it, Fred," I
said gently and so sadly that he took a
long turn about before he spoke again.

He sat down, looked a long time at my busy hands, and said bluntly, —

"One year in the States would wind it all up."

"How? What?" I asked in surprise.

"Because, Pauline, because," he continued, "because in one year you could have a good, honest, straight American divorce; and then—and then—in one minute after that you could—"

"Could what?" I asked with dignity.

"Why, you could marry me, Pauline."

I do not mind always what Fred says, he is so like a brother, but this time I gave him an indignant look, dropped my embroidery frame and silk on the floor, and went inside.

Madame Conard likes Mr. Olcott and hates Don Luis, so of course she has encouraged him in this idea.

However, Fred was not ill-natured about it: he is as accommodating as ever, and has engaged himself to do a very important little service for me in Curaçoa.

    *   *   *   *   *   *

October 10. I have just received a

letter from Fred Olcott, which he has managed to forward to me by a little coasting vessel, the *Alice*. Fred had to anchor the *Petrel* at Porta Plata to get some goods from his storehouse, and he has been caught there by a blockade and a revolution. We have been hearing rumors of it before, but the Conards were not excited, for rumors of revolution are frequently in the air here. But this seems to be the real thing, and I will copy Fred's account for you:

I am sorry to tell you, my little friend, that we are in the midst of a very serious revolution. This place has been besieged by the rebels for the past week. We have had several battles in the streets of the town. Each night we lie down, not knowing but that before morning the place will be in flames.

I dare not open my store for dread of pillage. We foreigners have to protect our own interests. I, with a number of others, have had to stand sentinel by night and help patrol the town. A battle has been fought at Santiago.

This town is filled with the wounded from the country.

Besides blockading our business, the government is calling on us merchants for money and food for the troops.

While I write you, shot and shell are flying over the town from the fort on the hill above to keep the rebels at bay.

The town people have to flock into the brick stores as the balls pass unobstructed through the wooden houses.

So you see, I am not unfurling my sails on the broad seas to speed away on your commission. But I will get away as soon as I can. I would rather be anywhere than here. This balmy climate, and those vernal shores, and three revolutions a year may suit the natives; but give me a safe home in the States and — well now — forgive me, dear, a New England wife. And of that last hope my envious heart will never be quite free.

*   *   *   *   *   *

October 20. — Still, my sister, I draw the threads in and out over my embroidery, and wait and hope for news from

San Domingo. Mr. Conard gives me some hope. He thinks the revolutionists are likely to succeed, and in the probability of such an event, the court is likely to be a little cautious.

He thinks, also, that the work of Mr. Hubbard, my adviser in New York, has had the object of retarding the efforts of de Castro to push the matter through under the present administration.

Fred Olcott is still detained at Porta Plata.

During the revolutionary excitement we remain very closely at the Adela Villa on the hill. But we can look down over the town, and see something of whatever happens to be going on.

The consul says that Don Luis, for some reason of his own, takes sides with the revolutionists, while Lavandier is for the existing government. The servants report that they have high words about it sometimes in the warehouses.

Don Luis hates an open quarrel, and it must be after these times that I see him walking by a long, low stone wall that bounds the Conard property on the south. It is a lonely path, and I see him passing and repassing in a slow, meditative walk.

Sometimes he is there when a shower comes up, and he is then gone long enough only to get his cloak.   Then I can still see his tall form dimly through the drops.

With all the perplexity and pain of my life, I was patient to wait upon his will, his desires, his ambition.

But this restlessness of his unnerves me.   Once he was there in the moonlight. It seemed to me the same moonlight that shone on the deck of the *Yarrow*.   I left the balcony, and something stronger than my will carried me (though I tried to remain) down toward the wall; I knew that my heart cried out, "He is suffering."

But rapid feet followed me, and Adela caught me by the arm.

"For shame!" she said, "let him come to you — you shall not."

She led me back; I knew she was right.

Even if he should come for all the trouble to be forgiven and forgotten, I know very well that my heart would rise up in rebellion against that mad, unreasonable jealousy of Portola.

And so the tears drop into my floss as I work the roses in my cushion, and my heart trembles within me, for I cannot forget my marriage day and all his tender devotion at Curaçoa.

*   *   *   *   *   *

October 24.   We have had an exciting time, so exciting to me that I forgot my own troubles for a while.   Three days ago Samaná was turned over to the revolutionists.

The Conards have seen so much of the same thing before on these islands, that they were not much excited or disturbed.

The revolutionists, who took this place, were largely composed of people who were living here, and were so greatly in the majority that the resistance was but a sham.

A band of men went out to meet the revolutionists, who would have been few, but for this reinforcement.

It was eleven o'clock at night when we

heard them firing in the distance. The governor took a small band of men, went out, challenged the advancing party, and fired a few rounds without hurting any one. Then the revolutionists came on rapidly, firing in the air, and shouting at the top of their voices.

This firing and shooting they kept up till they had taken the fort and all the guard posts of the town. No one was killed or hurt; but the American Consulate, being on an elevation, seemed to be getting all the balls. Several of them struck the house, and we could hear plenty of them go tap, tap, through the banana leaves.

While the balls were flying Adela made me lie flat on the floor; but she was up and down, laughing and enjoying it, as if it might have been a comedy on the stage.

Since then all has been quiet, and the actors in the fight laugh together in the streets.

But Lavandier is raging; he was in high favor with the party that has been deposed.

The Padre has been up to tell us about it. He says that the governor made his resistance a sham, partly because he hates the Señor Lavandier so much on account of his wicked treatment of me. The revolutionists will give the governor full credit for his conduct, and will probably keep him in office. How the good old Padre laughed over it! Madame Conard made him some coffee, and he hurried down the hill, his long cassock flapping in the wind as he walked.

*　　*　　*　　*　　*　　*

October 27. The revolution has been a success; the news has just come that the ex-president, the leader of the revolution, is now at San Domingo and in power. God has sent the revolution, — now pray to Him that it will help my case at the court of San Domingo.

*　　*　　*　　*　　*　　*

I do not often go to the House of Palms; since the decree of the Samaná judge I have been there but once to remain, and that was to receive Mercedes. So I do not have my maid Julia, but several times lately she has been up here with a small basket, filled with fruit or flowers, poised on her head. And very pretty she looks, too, — like a bronze statue, — with her smooth, polished arms stretched up, and her firm round ankles looking like metal under her short skirt. She always puts the basket down by me with a smile and a soft twinkle of her eye, but I cannot make her tell me who sent it.

Madame Conard always frowns when she sees her coming : I think from this that she associates it with Don Luis.

*　　*　　*　　*　　*　　*

October 23.　How strange life is, dear Nell! Sunshine follows shadow. Pleasure follows pain, just as I see the vernal hills here break all in one moment from the purple sea clouds and shine like green emeralds in the sun. But I have willed it that the clouds shall return. I cannot accept the love light that is so beautiful to me.

But I will tell you. There has been more or less ill feeling on account of the revolution, and the Señor Lavandier has had trouble with friends and foes. Some one has taken advantage of the unsettled state of affairs to break his power. His property is gone.

This morning we were awakened by a bright light coming through the open shutters. Immediately Madame Conard burst into my room.

"Such a grand fire! Come, come, Pauline!" she cried. We hurried out and then on to the upper balcony. The two warehouses belonging to Lavandier and Don Luis were in flames.

Adela is so excitable. She danced around, clapping her hands.

"Good! Me alegro mucho! I am very glad. You are avenged!" she cried.

But my heart trembled. My husband is not well; he will suffer from the excitement — besides, he needs his home, his comforts.

It was an awful scene to me. It was a destruction of valuable property and of many months' supplies for the surrounding country.

P

All was being wiped out in a moment.
A crowd of dark forms stood around in
the glare of the flames, but nothing could
be done to save such old wooden buildings.

Another light came over the palms. I
knew that there was oil stored in a little
palenca in the shrubbery. The fire was
there; the explosion threw burning bits
all over the House of Palms.

I turned sick and faint. That was the
end of my dreams of a home by the sea
—a home of love, hospitality, and ease,
where I might have met and entertained
all of the intellectual foreign residents of
the island and all the interesting strangers.

I thought of the lovely things that had
been brought from New York for me,
and the library, full of old Spanish,
French, and English books, and rare
curios.

Thus while regret feasted on my dreams
and memories, the flames scorched and
curled the great feathery palms.

When daylight came I went and cor-

rected my hasty toilet, had coffee with the
Conards, then returned to the upper balcony; while Adela, who wished to be in
the excitement of the hour, and get all the
news, went down to the town with her
husband.

While standing there and observing
what I could through the openings of the
intervening trees, I heard quick steps
come through the house, up the stairs,
and out on the balcony.

I thought of Fred Olcott. I turned.
It was Don Luis.

But such a satisfied and joyous expression on his face! Then my anger colored my cheek. I knew that some words
had passed his lips to the Padre in regard
to the Señor Don Juan Portola. I re-
sented that bitterly. I was amazed at his
bold appearance there; I stood looking
toward him in silent scorn.

He was looking at me with the old
kindly light in his eyes.

Then he took my hand gently. I was
thrilled at the touch — I was helpless.
He led me down into Adela's little par-

lor.   He handed me to a chair as gracefully and as calmly as he alone can do
such things.

"Look at me as scornfully as you
please," he said; "it rather becomes you.
I am going to talk to you. Do you know
what this fire means, little Condesa?   Do
you know what it means?   It means that
there is nothing more to manœuvre for —
it means that I am free.   Free, darling!
The Venezuela bonds — the last thing I
have been trying to get out of my schem-
ing partner, by treating my American wife
so shamefully — have gone out of existence in this smoke.

"You do not know the extent of that
man's plots.   He thought he could get
rid of you — get you out of the country
and marry me, in place of my dead son,
to his daughter.   My counterplot was
to get the property, the bonds, and my
wife, too.   Now it is all over and I am
free!

"It was a costly fire, but I am paid.
Come, mia Condesa.   I am poor, I have
only my little estate in Spain: we owe

that to the suit.   Lavandier was so un-
wary as to free it from debt, when he
gained the suit against you.   Felix is the
heir — you do not care for that; you
will love him, too.   I have a few thousand
dollars in a bank at New Orleans.   Let
us go away from here.   Come, Pauline,
let us forget the shame, the misery of the
past."   He extended his arms in the old
way, so magnetic, so strangely fascinating.   But I resisted, I do not know
how, by walking away to the other side of
the room.   I trembled.   It was some
moments before I dared to speak.

"No, no, no," I said, "I cannot come
back to you!   The judge of Samaná has
declared that I am not your wife.   Besides," and I dared to look boldly at
him then, "I could not accept the Señor
Portola's dishonest attentions; if you
think I could, Don Luis, you need me no
more for a wife.   The court has decreed
well.   Let it stand.   In the name of my
country-women I must resent an insult of
that kind."

I leaned against the wall and hid my

face in my hands.   He was silent till I
grew calm, then I looked up.

"Dear child," he said very gently,
"every one knows how that suit was won.
It amounts to nothing.

"But as to the other, I confess that I
have weak attacks.   I am nervous, both
mentally and physically.   You know that
I have never been jealous of Olcott—only
to envy him his many privileges.   But
on my arrival from Curaçoa, I was tired,
worn, discouraged, and Lavandier poured
into my ear the gossip de Castro had
manufactured for him.   I thought of my
ill treatment of you; I thought of his
powers of fascination.

"But it was only in a moment of weakness.   My first sight of your proud face
at the Padre's house drove it from my
mind.

"See, here is a letter that the Señor
Portola has written me.   He says the
revolution has lost him his case at San
Domingo, and I will gain you yours, for
everything is changed.   In a postscript he
asks me why I am so unkind to my wife.

He says you are the most lovely and
virtuous woman he ever knew, and that
you won the respect of all San Domingo.

"I did not need him to tell me that. I
consider him beneath my notice.

"Dearest little Pauline, I know this has
hurt you; but let us forget it. Can you
not forgive me?"

Much as I rejoiced, my dear sister,
that he should be at my feet, my soul re-
volted against all the unkind treatment I
had received, and against the sufferings
and dangers I had passed through.

I drew myself up with all the haughti-
ness I could command, but I did not
trust myself to speak. I lifted my arm
and pointed to the door — I was proud
of my power to punish him.

He cast his eyes down; it seemed a
long time before he spoke. Then he
rose with an unsteady movement, holding
his hand firmly over his heart.

"It causes me great suffering to sit and
talk to you of this," he said, but, oh, so
patiently and kindly! "I will not prolong the interview. You will repent of

this, Pauline. I will speak to the Padre, he will help us." He walked to the door; then he turned with a smile, and a bit of his old irresistible wit, —

"I see you are not a doll-wife, after all, as I said at your wedding, to be tossed about as one pleases."

He went out, and I let him go! I threw myself on the sofa, and sobbed till Adela came.

My dear sister, this is the sunlight on the hill that the cloud comes over. It gives me great joy to know that the man to whom I am married loves me still; but I do not know what I am living for. Everything seems a blank.

The consul has written a fresh batch of letters to the new government at San Domingo. If I could get that dreadful decree reversed, and if good Mr. Olcott should find those jewels, my name would be free of every stain. I could come home then; but — but — I don't know what I should want to do, *then*.

PAULINE.

Chapter XVIII

"And Always Their Padre"

(The Padre's Notes)

October 27. I am ever at the call of friend, foe, and strangers. There is no service the curate of Samaná is not supposed to be willing to do.

But I am more than willing to do the last services (whatever they may be) for my little American friend, and to continue my record of her life's chapter on this island.

The day that the warehouses burned, I looked about anxiously for Don Luis, knowing of his tendency to suffer physically from excitement. But I was unable to find him. But at nightfall a boatman brought me a note from him. I followed its directions and went down through the desolate fire-scorched palm garden, and

found Don Luis seated in the canopied boat.

"Come, Dr. Caccavelli," he said very
pleasantly, "you will enjoy a little boating with me. Have a seat and a cigar."

It was a fine night and a bright moon,
so I took the seat opposite. There were
various light personal effects stored about,
and Don Luis ordered the one boatman
to row out slowly to the English steamer,
which had anchored in the bay that afternoon.

"We will speak in French, Padre," he
said to me, "for I do not want this fellow
to know my business. You know that
everything is ended for me here. If
Lavandier wishes to rebuild and own the
business, he may. I am sick of this fight
for money, and I am thinking now of
trying to prolong my miserable life. I
did not think before that life was so
precious. My ambition is gone. I am
content now to have life alone, and — and
— the countess, Padre. I want to leave
some charges with you, and I will tell
you my plans. This steamer will land

me at San Domingo where I will do
what I can to have my wife win the
empty honor of her suit. Then I will
go over to New Orleans, and then to
California. I believe the climate there is
the only one for me. I was there before
I went to New England, and I thought
I was cured of — of — this weakness :
you know what I mean, my dear Padre.

" The clear, dry air there is what I need.
Now I want to leave her with you. She
thinks she cannot forgive me for my
jealousy, for all that I have caused her
to suffer. I agree with her. It was a
contemptible ambition ; but what Lavandier controlled was my life's work.
Padre, you know I wanted to get what
I could out of it. She will feel different
when that decree is reversed. Her anger
will fade out ; she loved me once. I leave
it all with you. You can influence her.
Work upon her pity, her charity. Tell
her I am a sufferer, a weak sufferer, if
you wish. Love is akin to pity. See
that star fall. Well, my lamp of life
may go out any moment like that. You

may tell her. Her mercy will be my best medicine — tell her that, Padre.

"That Olcott, that upstart, will never find those jewels. But if he should, they are hers; make her keep them, whether she comes to me or not. But, Padre, she will come; don't you think so? There is one thing more, if I should never see her again," his voice failed here, "if anything should happen, write to my lawyer in Spain, here's the address — she will never want to go to that miserable little estate, but she must be acknowledged as my countess (if she wins her case), — and you will see to it, won't you?" And I gave him my promise.

He said much more. He was sensible of all I had done; that he deemed my great goodness.

"Your character is my religion; there'll be time yet to renew my faith in your creed," he said. I implored him not to postpone the sacred hour. He gave me many directions and messages for his wife. He would send me a check for her from New Orleans; he would write every mail, if I would give her the messages. I begged him to return and say a last word to friends, who had loved him before, and would love him again. But he said he must continue to avoid excitement. So I gave him my farewell at the steamer's side, and came home.

November 20. The last *Coceta de Santo Domingo,* the official organ of the Dominican government, gave two columns to the case of the Señora de Curzoñ. The Supreme Corte de Justicia revokes in all its parts the judgment of the Tribunal del Distrito Judicial de Santa Barbará de Samaná, and pronounces legal la demanda (the demand) of the legal esposa (wife). The new government evidently knows no Señor Lavandier. I have been walking the street and reading the *Gazeta* to friend and foe.

Captain Gavard and Julian are nowhere to be seen. They had not counted on the downfall of their master, or on a possible revolution.

The Señora de Curzoñ is as happy as a child. I have not yet approached her with the delicate mission entrusted to me by Don Luis. It is best that this event should have full time to have its effect on her mind. Then when I have told her all, I doubt not that the charity of her woman's heart will open up the old tides of tenderness, and that love will dictate to her a line of duty.

*   *   *   *   *   *

November 21. The young American, Olcott of the *Petrel,* walked into my room last evening, and demanded that I should go trudging up Conard's hill for the countess. Remembering my promise to Don Luis to guard her movements faithfully, I did so, and brought her down.

When she had given him, I thought, an exceedingly friendly greeting, he laid a crumpled velvet spread on the table, and produced in various packets from about his person the jewelry, stones, and precious things that had been described to me. Olcott said :

" The poor old creature, Sheba, had but one theme, and that was, ' the poor little wife of Curzoñ! Lavandier will kill her!' I told her I knew all about it, and that he would spare her life for a handful of red stones and a bracelet. This pleased her very much (and it pleased me that I spoke such intelligible French), and she went on in high glee, while I walked on the air at her heels. She went down to the wall a ways and took the bundle from behind a stone, where any black urchin might have found it. That night I added the whole to my handful, and set sail."

The Señor Olcott would accept no thanks from the countess, not even the gorgeous ruby she held out to him, begging him to accept it for her sake. He shook his head, and thrusting both hands in his pockets stood looking silently at the floor.

Presently I was ready, and we saw the countess and her treasures safely under the roof of the Consulate.

The American seemed not so bold and

self-assured as he was before he went away.
Probably he realizes that this very plain
though innocent courtship of the señora,
the countess, cannot be renewed. But he
is a brave and clever young man, and I
think not ill of him.

December 1. A very tragic event has
occurred in the little city of Samaná. Last
Saturday night the wretched Julian Carlos
was called before the Tribunal of Jesus
Christ, there to render a strict account of
his conduct.

I knew that he had injured himself by
heavy lifting on the night of the fire, and
later I understood that he had had an
attack of hemorrhage of the lungs, and
was ill in a palenca out by the forest.

I had no call to interest myself in the
matter, however, and did not until Fri-
day morning, when Margarite came to
me in a condition of abject sorrow.
Kneeling at my feet, and wetting my
gown with her tears, she begged me to
save her. I looked with contempt and
pity on the unhappy girl.

"Did I not warn you?" I said.

"Oh, good Padre, yes, yes," she sobbed; "but come now! He is willing to marry me before he dies. Come, before it is too late. When my little one comes, I will be Madame Carlos."

I lifted the prostrate girl from the floor, gave her a stimulant, and we went to the bedside of her false and wicked lover.

He seemed gratified at my appearance, and roused up his strength to go through the marriage ceremony. Then I told him that God would punish him for all his evil deeds. He seemed not to be capable of true repentance, but before I came away, he said,—

"The sin that weighs most heavily on my conscience is my injustice to the good countess."

"You well know," I answered, "that you have been paid as you deserve. You followed a wicked master: such a one could not reward you well. Besides, you abandoned the crushed Margarite, hoping to gain Mercedes. May God and Margarite forgive you, I cannot."

Q

Later, I thought better of my harshness and went again. He was better; he had forgotten his sins; he needed no priest. He was happy with Margarite.

But Saturday evening his hemorrhage returned. The warning was the last. He died miserably. I was sent for, but arrived too late.

"Verily," I said as I came away, "the wages of sin is Death."

December 14. The dear young American lady, the Countess of Villemaceda, took passage on the English steamer to-day, en route to California to join her husband.

She begged to be allowed to take Mercedes and Felix. Bah! She might as well take a whole island hacienda as that indolent and extravagant beauty. But before I had convinced her of her folly, we were relieved of the whole matter by Captain Gavard, who sailed away one night with Mercedes and Felix to Porta Plata where, it is said, he intends to marry her.

Nothing remained but for me to say a

mass for the Countess of Villemaceda, my friend, and pray for her safety on land and sea.

With her dark eyes wide open and wondering, she knelt with Madame Conard and took part, as well as she was able, in the ceremonies.

The best people of Samaná accompanied us to the beach, where she said her frank, simple " good-by " to them all.

Several boat loads of friends went out to the steamer, and standing on the deck the consul, his wife, and I bade her farewell. Poor Madame Conard wept hysterically. I myself felt moved. I gave her my blessing while she knelt at my feet, and thanked me again and again for what I had done for her. I gave her a simple little gold cross, as a memento of me. She put it to her lips, and her tears fell over it, as we pushed our boat away.

On shore my people gathered about me to gratify a natural curiosity as to her plans. I told them of her destination, and took occasion to speak of the greatness of the United States, and the nobility and intelligence of its people. I said that I had always desired greatly to become a resident of that country, but that I now had no ambition but to do my fullest duty to the people of Samaná, while I would always be courteous to strangers, that I was none the less always their devoted Padre.

Here the men, as with one movement, uncovered their heads respectfully, and we dispersed to our several duties.

Chapter XIX

At Hotel Del Monte

(A Letter)

OAKLAND, CALIFORNIA,
Feb. 28, 18–.

THE DOCTOR CACCAVELLI, Curate of
Samaná,

DEAR PADRE : — After many days I sit
down to write you more fully of what you
know somewhat from my short notes
from time to time.

Just now, dear friend, I am in the
lovely city of Oakland — a place of homes
and flowers.

I have found New England friends
here, and amid these ever-blooming gar-
dens I am resting with a new peace upon
my heart : peace that God has given me.
And I thank Him, and you, dear Padre,
every day for the sweet hours that came
to me in this fair land after my year of
trouble and distress.

I found Don Luis, after my long trip through the Rocky Mountains, waiting for me at the pleasant town of Auburn, a sunny, rocky hillside place on the western slope of the Sierras.

He did not rise from his chair to meet me, and my heart failed when I saw how much he had changed.

I was grieved, then, that I had not yielded at Samaná, and come with him. I felt reproached.

I stood hesitating, and as soon as the attendant had gone from the room I knelt at his feet, weeping bitterly.

"O Don Luis," I cried, "what have I done? I was cruel not to come. Forgive me, forgive me! You are ill!"

I could say no more for my sobs.

Then he took away my hat and wrap, and caressed my hair softly and tenderly, saying but once, —

"There is nothing to forgive, dear little Condesa, — let there be nothing, — it is only to forget!"

He let me kneel there till I was calm, and my heart ceased to beat so wildly.

Then he kissed my hand and drew me to his side.

"Mio beloved, do you remember," he said after a while, "what Captain Benton read on deck of the *Yarrow*, 'If I take the wings of the morning and dwell in the uttermost parts of the sea,' and about the right hand? Surely, we have come to the uttermost parts of the sea, and you are still in His right hand. You are so good, I believe you could not sin. Do you think your God would forgive me for all, for everything?"

Then I wound my arm about his neck; I would not let him speak so — I kissed away the words.

He asked about you first of all, dear Padre. He smiled when I told him that Mr. Olcott did not come to the ship to see me off.

When I told him of Julian, he made no remarks. "He was a good servant," he said, that was all.

But he was truly distressed about Mercedes and Felix.

He wrote a note at once to his lawyer

in Spain ; the lawyer there will write you in regard to Felix.

They will want you to see that he is educated with due regard to his future rights and inheritance.

Then we resolved to go out of the shadows of the past, and live for ourselves alone.

In the hours that followed he gained strength, and was like himself again. We used to walk out on the long porch of the rambling old hotel, and the fresh air from the rugged red mountains gave him new life.

All my hope returned when he was able to ride horseback with me over the rocky roads, to breathe the strengthening aroma from the sweet pines.

He seemed quite as he was when I first met him. We began to be glad of every day and hour of life; and he told me often that I had kept my promise to atone for his barren, wasted life.

The guests at the hotel called us the handsome count and the gay little countess.

But he wearied of the primitiveness of
the surroundings there, and the appoint-
ments of the place were not luxurious
enough to suit his tastes, so we came
down to Hotel del Monte, — a palatial
hotel on the Bay of Monterey, which,
but for the absence of islands, is so like
the Bay of Samaná.

Here we drove among the odorous red-
woods and walked in the luxuriant garden,
where the frailest tropical blossoms rise
up in the shade of the mossy oaks. We
could sit on the beach also, and I thought
so often of a golden sunset I had seen on
the Bay of Samaná, where a path of glory
stretched prophetically out to the west.
This, then, was the end to that path of
glory — a path dazzling in its brightness
till it was cut off in a moment.

He rose one morning earlier than usual,
and went out in the garden alone. I
found him later in a rustic seat under an
oak, and when I saw him I thought of
that day in Martinique when I first saw
him in a faint attack.

But he seemed not so very ill, and we

walked slowly back to our room. On the way he said to me:

"Could I not go to San Francisco, and sell some more of those jewels, so we could send for the Padre? I would like to see that grand old man once more."

I told him nothing would please me better than to see that noble face again.

Then he spoke of Felix, and when in our parlor he sat down in a reclining chair, and said he used to write French verses, and that if I would push up a writing-table, he would try to write something about Felix.

With a smile on his face he began to write. Soon after I came out of my dressing-room, and saw that a great change had come. I rang for help. He knew me, but presently ceased to breathe.

His last words were, " My dear wife, mia Condesa ! "

You will be glad to know, dear Padre, that he had been to confession several times, so I sent for the priest, and he was very kind.

And so, at the end at that path of light, I was left alone ; *and it was very dark.*

PAULINE DE CURZOÑ,
The Countess of Villemaceda.

.

.

THE END